GLUTTONY

7 Deadly Sins Vol. 2

First published as a collection June 2018

Content copyright © Pure Slush Books and individual authors
Edited by Matt Potter

All rights reserved by the authors and publisher. Except for brief excerpts used for review or scholarly purposes, no part of this book may be reproduced in any manner whatsoever without express written consent of the publisher or the author/s.

Pure Slush Books
32 Meredith Street
Sefton Park SA 5083
Australia

Email: edpureslush@live.com.au
Website: https://pureslush.com/
Store: https://pureslush.com/store/

Original plate photograph copyright © Michal Zacharzewski
Cover design copyright © Matt Potter

ISBN: 978-1-925536-54-6

Also available as an eBook
ISBN: 978-1-925536-55-3

A note on differences in punctuation and spelling

Pure Slush Books proudly features writers from all over the English-speaking world. Some speak and write English as their first language, while for others, it's their second or third or even fourth language. Naturally, across all versions of English, there are differences in punctuation and spelling, and even in meaning. These differences are reflected in the work *Pure Slush Books* publishes, and accounts for any differences in punctuation, spelling and meaning found within these pages.

Pure Slush Books is a member of the
Bequem Publishing collective
http://www.bequempublishing.com/

• Edward AHERN • Alan C. BAIRD • Elaine BARNARD • Paul BECKMAN • Jon BENNETT • Howard BROWN • Michael H. BROWNSTEIN • Mark BUDMAN • Steven CARR • Guilie CASTILLO ORIARD • CHANGMING Yuan • Jan CHRONISTER • Marcia CONOVER • Carolyn CORDON • Judah Eli CRICELLI • Ruth Z. DEMING • Andrea DIEDE • Salvatore DiFALCO • Michael ESTABROOK • Tom FEGAN • Nod GHOSH • Ken GOSSE • Roberta GOULD • Steven GOWIN • Noah GRABEEL • Anne GRAUE • Jake GREENBLOT • Andrew GRENFELL • Shane GUTHRIE • Jan HAAG • Louise HOFMEISTER • Sharron HOUGH • Mark HUDSON • Abha IYENGAR • Bryan JANSING • Jemshed KHAN • Linda KOHLER • John KUJAWSKI • John LAMBREMONT Sr. • Ron LAVALETTE • Valerie LAWSON • Tracy LEE-NEWMAN • Larry LEFKOWITZ • Cynthia LESLIE-BOLE • Peter LINGARD • JP LUNDSTROM • Chuck MADANSKY • Karla Linn MERRIFIELD • Marsha MITTMAN • Leah MUELLER • Piet NIEUWLAND • Carl 'Papa' PALMER • Melisa QUIGLEY • Dorothy RICE • Joanne RIZZO • Ruth Sabath ROSENTHAL • Sarah SALWAY • Shawn Aveningo SANDERS • Rikki SANTER • Wayne SCHEER • Iris N. SCHWARTZ • Fraser SUTHERLAND • Lucy TYRRELL • Marian URQUILLA • Rob WALKER • Townsend WALKER • Rob WALTON • Michael WEBB • Jeffrey WEISMAN •

Contents

1   Poetry

65   Prose

Poetry

Poetry

5	Ossobucco	*Valerie Lawson*
6	Gelato	*Michael Estabrook*
7	The perfect meal	*Rob Walker*
8	Comfort	*Melisa Quigley*
9	A Different Kind of Light	*Chuck Madansky*
10	Beads in New Orleans	*Lucy Tyrrell*
12	Over Hungry	*Shane Guthrie*
13	Anniversary of Eve	*Jan Chronister*
14	Dessert	*Jan Haag*
16	A River	*Piet Nieuwland*
18	An American Appetite	*Carl 'Papa' Palmer*
19	Leftovers	*Fraser Sutherland*
20	Oh my …	*Marsha Mittman*
21	Anything Goes	*Karla Linn Merrifield*
22	Gluttony Curtailed	*Ruth Sabath Rosenthal*
24	The Injustice of Cheesecake	*Anne Graue*
27	A Big Appetite	*John Lambremont Sr.*
28	Proclamation from The Diet of Gluttony	*Ken Gosse*
30	Ravenous	*Leah Mueller*
32	Our Garden	*Michael H. Brownstein*
34	Club Gluttony	*Ruth Z. Deming*

35	Cyberfood	*Roberta Gould*
36	Gluttony	*Howard Brown*
38	Thin Lines	*Rikki Santer*
40	*Chi* (Eat): Insight into Chinese Civilization *Changming Yuan*	
41	Lucky to Be Here	*Jon Bennett*
42	Saving Lives	*Carolyn Cordon*
44	Fat City	*Louise Hofmeister*
46	Kummerspeck	*Marian Urquilla*
48	Forbidden Fruit	*Joanne Rizzo*
50	Oblivious	*Marcia Conover*
53	I like you for the way fruit pops in your mouth. *Linda Kohler*	
54	Teacups, Teacups– Everywhere ... and Not a Scone in Sight *Shawn Aveningo Sanders*	
56	Fat Ronald Cheats	*Ron Lavalette*
58	Feast or Fast	*Mark Hudson*
62	Invisible Trenches Between Me And My Other Self *Judah Eli Cricelli*	

Ossobucco

Valerie Lawson

Rose fed veal makes the dish,
choice-cut top of the shank
five inches across, two inches thick.
Leave the skin to hold it together.
Let the soffritto take its time.

Dredge, sauté, arrosto morto—
turn the meat, braise tenderly.
Plunder the spice road: nutmeg,
cloves, cinnamon—saffron
for the risotto excites the tongue.

Oss bus, hollow bone, marrow mouth
lends a velvet shine to the sauce.
Gremalatto cuts the sweetness
with zest. Costasera Amarone
to wash down humble cucina.

Fine linen tucked at the chin
to catch the dripping grease
the back of the hand smears
more on red bloated cheeks
the curse of deep hunger.

Gelato

Michael Estabrook

"I just realized that Michelangelo's David
is the David who slays Goliath
in the Bible," says John
his face beaming.
My eyes widen
as I realize not everyone
on this tour of Venice, Florence and Rome
is here for the art, history and culture.
I also realize that rather
than learning about these things
these people are here
to spend their money on gold jewelry
leather goods, wine and Murano glass
to see olive trees and vineyards
and eat Mozzarella Fritta, Antipasto, Calamari
Gamberi Spiedo, Bruschetta, Penne al Pomodoro
Tortelloni All'aragosta, Rigatoni con Luganega
Spaghetti alla Bolognese, Porcini Agnolotti
Gnocchi di Sorrento, Ravioli al Pomodoro
Pollo Parmigiano, Filetto Balsamico
Vitello Piccata, Panna Cotta, Torta di Formaggio
Mousse di Cioccolato Torta, Tiramisu
Coppa di Gelato Guarnita
topped off with an Espresso
and a glass of delicious Courvoisier Cognac.

The perfect meal

Radisson Blue, Fiji

Rob Walker

A symphony of fish and prawns
with Indonesian spices, lychees, lime.
(Perhaps the Massaman Sir might prefer?)
Optimism briefly dawns.
A handsome cast
a waiting staff who flatter and defer
in smooth utterings. Take your time!
The menu is diverse and vast.

Red lips and brilliant blue sarong,
white hibiscus tucked in midnight hair.
But non-core promises soon go dry.
The menu is misleading, wrong,
a dodgy deal.
The proffered discount card does not apply.
The signature dish just isn't there.
Like fishbones in your throat, this meal…

Comfort

Melisa Quigley

Staring at your picture
on the mantlepiece
picking it up
and holding it close
now life's not the same
Watching you wither
made my appetite wane
Since you've been gone
I'm gourmandising on food
People think I'm happy
but I'm a landslide inside
A friend called me a glutton
which I found very rude
If she only knew how I felt
she would understand
food is my saviour
it nurtures and comforts
where no one else can

A Different Kind of Light

Chuck Madansky

When I've eaten all the chips,
I write it on the list,
and soon there will be more.
This more has followed me from birth.
The earth has tilted just so,
has shaken the not-so-much,
the less, the never, onto other lives,
other lists. I have visited
their houses and bare shelves,
their cardboard on the street grates,
and handed "some" to them,
knowing there was always more.

O, the secret price of more—
blankets laced with smallpox,
produce picked for pennies,
blue jeans sewn in chains.

Torches lead the way
to keep the world
on tilt to more…
we need a different kind
of light to say
Enough.

Beads in New Orleans

Lucy Tyrrell

I walk from trolley to café.
Azaleas paint gardens
pink, white.
Camellias scatter
fading cups of color
on the sidewalk.
Beads abandoned after Mardi Gras
dangle from sharp spears
of wrought-iron fences—
gold for power
purple for justice
green for faith.

Seated at curved counter
in Camellia Grill,
I fork chocolate pecan pie
bite by bite, piece by piece—
syrupy sweetness, nutty crunch,
smooth dark melt.

For my pie indulgence,
I should festoon myself
with strings of beads—
but of a color other than
green, purple, gold.
Where can I find strands
of corpulent beads—
orange for gluttony?

Over Hungry

Shane Guthrie

I've done some stress eating at parties
I'll admit it
Dumb, but not a sin

I've eaten a single messy faceful of cake
Before throwing the whole thing away

I've read everything an author has published
Then found out he was dead and cried
But not from guilt

I asked for every story your youth could deliver
Every broken bone and high-school rumor
Every sled ride and first kiss
Every shameful thing that turned you on

That was sweeter than sugar

But the way I called too much
The way I asked for your time
then demanded, then begged
Before you refused another word

That was pure gluttony

Anniversary of Eve

Jan Chronister

The apple I ate
weighs heavy inside
and the premature summer night
leads to wild thoughts of
sweat-shiny bodies
already another year older.

I'm trying to starve my mind
but my gluttony only increases
when I see the serpent in the
form of one of
last year's suppers.

Dessert

Jan Haag

On those balmy June evenings
I became your Charlotte of pears,
you my summer berry grunt,

and we could not get enough.

We became gluttons,
a rhubarb mess,
tiny raspberry fools

who found it difficult
to weather the warm days
until our arms could
reach for each other—

orange buckle,
treacle sponge—

an endless dessert,
often without dinner first,
as dusk came on.

You, my black bun
I, your pond pudding

inhaling the sweetness
at the bottom of the pie
before licking the plate clean

sticky fingers in mouths,
giggles erupting from
satiated throats, from
over-sweetened tongues

the newly discovered nectar,
the intoxicating trifle
of us.

A River

Piet Nieuwland

Sinusoidal, breathing into the delta
Wet coiled oxbows, silt mosaics, fields, plots and gardens
Fertility for kumara, spinach, tomatoes, garlic and beans
The immaculate process of bee laden pollenating wind
Saturated air fresh with spring rains
Absorbing into fragile root tissues, the breathing soil
A flourish in tensile light, of sky that turns kingfisher blue
Exciting arcades of chloroplast platters
Vibrant expressions of bright red tomato and pomegranate love
Joyous oranges, carrots and persimmons
Beans and aubergines, their rich purple lust
Potato happiness,
Served with fresh mullet, broccoli and mustard
Olive oils, avocado flesh,
Scented with sage, coriander and basil
Breads, leavened, kneaded,
The daily ritual of yeasty aromas baked
Sliced, with honeys and jam, soft cheeses, nuts and dates
All life is food and all food is life, the taste web
The raw, uncooked, fermented, fried, grilled, roasted
Fresh, frozen, preserved, pickled, dried
Statements of culture, vitality and tastes,
The spiced, salty, sweet sauces

Our obsession, the whole grains we eat
The food forest of the island planet
Sacred summer barbeque in the shade
We are eating the world and all that lives in it
It is all our food, the food of humans
The jungles, the fruit, the nuts and berries
Its oceans, the plankton, what they eat, what eats them
The tuna and shellfish, pelagic schools of herrings
Lakes and rivers, their trout, salmon, eel, koura
The air, the chickens, their eggs, the ducks and insects
Rich black soils of mushrooms, tubers, fungi
It is all our food, the drinks, the juices, alcohols, and teas
The tastes, smells, what we need for the day
What the earth gives us, gives us,
The billions of us, to swallow

An American Appetite

Carl 'Papa' Palmer

Eating here stateside is hard to define.
Much more than cheese wedgies, veggies and meat,
or drive-thru fast foods on most any street.
Choosing food from signs while waiting in line,
we "dress to the nines" with waiters and wine,
snack between meal treats of anything sweet,
on a bar stool seat, sit waiting to eat.
It can be fine not to dine by design.
We eat with our hands at hamburger stands.
We graze the buffet while filling our tray.
From various brands, from various lands,
from breakfast soufflé, to evening sorbet,
our waists expand as we "munch on demand."
We eat "our way" here in the USA.

Leftovers

Fraser Sutherland

"I find that my Lhasa Apso, Sangfroid,
is a good repository for leftovers."
— *in a women's magazine*

With a Lhasa's or an Apso's appetite,
Sangfroid scoffs salmon mousse.
Well-feathered tail upcurled,
the dense-coated Tibetan garburator,
plunges into baked Alaska,
dark nose down into the meatloaf, deep in
veal parmigiana, yogurt and cucumber dip,
profiteroles, and lobster bisque.
Thus the solution to the perennial issue of
what you do with leftovers silting up your fridge
and the composter's top-heavy
and you can't afford to airfreight them to the Sahel starving
and you don't need the extra calories
and you just don't want to throw them out.
You don't have to!
You can feed them to your dog.

Oh my ...

Marsha Mittman

It sits there
Laughing at me
Mocking me
Sensing my excitement
My weakness, my gluttony
Whilst I contemplate
The sinfulness, the richness
Oh my gawd
The downright hedonism

Damn
Caution to the wind
Against all better judgement
I grab a spoon
And the jar of Nutella
And joyfully dig in…

Anything Goes

Karla Linn Merrifield

In a house with its pink
painted spiral stairway,
roofless bedroom, & milk
chocolate bathtub, she lives
alone, except for the gluttonous ghost
of her older brother & an
obese field mouse. Some say
she is a writer or a thrower
of pots. I know she masturbates
thrice daily, facing east, & chases
ladybugs into her garden. Tomorrow
she will kiss the shaggy mammoth
who sleeps in her garage & I will
befriend her, too, snorting joy.

Gluttony Curtailed

Ruth Sabath Rosenthal

This little piggy went to market — his Sicilian mamma
to the butcher. (*Do you suppose Pygmalion ever ate Italian?*)
& in an open-air market in Seville, one piggy oinked
to another, "How's it hangin"? "By the chinny-chin-chin

of chorizo," grunted the sow. "It's questionable how
it is with pig, but with dog, I hear life's a bitch." &
in the town of Pigskill, New York, during the annual
barbecue, one little piggy was the butt of ridicule

when he curtailed the cocktail hour by wolfing down
every last hors d'oeuvre. Round & round the mulberry
bush, a dog chased a pig & the pig chased a boy, till
all flopped down, bushed & squealing — ravenous —

the aroma of cracklin' heavy in the air, on their minds,
the main-event feeding frenzy in store. Uncle Meyer &
his cronies made total pigs of themselves & were told,
on no uncertain terms, that unless they swore not to

hog, in any way, shape or form,
any such future festivities, the swine would not be
given entry. So, the pig head honchos met & made
a pact to oversee that all their kind act appropriately.

It was not that long ago that a charge of the Pig Brigade caused quite a stink in the town — all barbecuing had come to a screeching halt & famished bikers had wrung their hands & popped Xanax. Only the Mayor could've kept the porkers from utter desperation, but, he'd skipped town at the first peal of the pig bell. When mayhem finally died down, the Mayor returned & explained away his absence with a tale of woe:

His best buddy had keeled over during his bachelor party. Evidentially, it was too much drink & mild food poisoning, not the dire emergency the Mayor had understood it to be. So, to save face, he called for a town hall meeting, at which time he announced that, if ever faced with another Pig Brigade invasion, he'd uphold the law of the land to the fullest extent. That was just what the townies needed to hear. Dissent derailed — all returned home feeling safe & content.

The Injustice of Cheesecake

Anne Graue

That it exists at all is cause
for concern—the German
confection—Bavarian born.
The naturally skinny claim

to love and eat it, and of course
I do and would devour as much
as possible when alone, willing,
just depressed enough.

The cheesecake melts in the 98
degree heat, me,
holding it there
as long as I can until
it slides down
slimy sweet promising
to stay with me always.

After 45 it is useless, the dieting;
LA, grapefruit, cabbage soup,
Weight Watchers, Atkins, no carbs,
low carbs, all protein, all water,
juice cleanse, drinking iced/hot water,
eating ice, taking vitamins, enduring
veggies, meat, no meat, fish that
swim forward.

Take all you want but eat all you take,
her father said at so many dinners—
meat, potatoes, salads, beans grown
out back, bread four for a dollar
from Kroger or Safeway.

How could she know if her eyes
were bigger than her stomach?
were bigger than her desire
to taste something that wasn't

nothing. In her room, in the mirror,
singing with Karen Carpenter,
she saw her body inside of her body
the one others couldn't see.
Eat less; it's *just* portion control.

Eat cabbage soup until you puke
up your insides. Take a pill, drink
a shake; Medifast, green tea, and cleanses
that drain her of time lost to counting
points, calories, and ounces
of Acai berry juice.

Eat the cactus fruit, the candied walnut,
the vasilopita.

Eat the ugali, the sukuma wiki, the samaki
na chapati.

Eat hamburgers, hot dogs, peach cobblers,
mashed potatoes and gravy, hotcakes
made by Midwestern pioneer women.

Eat all you want, but don't take another bite.

A Big Appetite
an acrostic

John Lambremont, Sr.

Gorge yourself like a mad bull in full rage;
Lessen your chances of reaching old age;
Upset your stomach and block your blood vessels.
'Til you are all flab and lacking in muscles;
Tell yourself one more time diets can wait,
Only to find out one day it's too late;
Near to exploding, with death at your door;
Yet, you have room for just one big meal more.

Proclamation from The Diet of Gluttony

Ken Gosse

This sin which blithely overwhelms
ensures disaster at our helms.
Gourmandic genes lie deep within
and fill us all with deep chagrin
while raging 'gainst that dark'ning diet—
tempting, teasing us to try it,
knowing well our failure rate—
lose ten, gain one, fall prostrate
then gorge ourselves in mournful sorrow,
still believing by the morrow
we'll resume this losing battle,
(never mind the aching rattle
of our appetites which beckon,
ache for bacon beyond reckon).

Yet, those few who do succeed
don't understand this vicious need
to look like them. Their ads, a vision
holding us to self-derision,
driving us, in deep despair
to buy more, eat more, they don't care
for they're paid well to demonstrate
the bodies we would emulate
from envy and, in fullest stride,
we hope to cultivate with pride.
For gluttony, should we atone,
is just one sin and not alone.

Ravenous

Leah Mueller

Hot donut holes
in a greasy white bag
fresh from the baker:
three kids, two adults
wait at home for breakfast.

Walking home fast
one sticky July morning,
I try not to look at
these succulent bulbs
of sugar and fat
pressed against my chest
like eager hands.

Breeze scent of corn
from nearby silos
competes with the
sweet glazed aroma.
Slowly, I peel open the bag,
stare at its labial folds.

Allowed just one
tiny bite on my walk,
I swallow seven more
in rapid, furtive gulps
like a drunk taking shots.

At home, I watch enviously
while the others chew,
and my parents demand
to know why I'm
always hungry, no matter
how much I eat.

Our Garden

Michael H. Brownstein

The autumn leaves fall where they land,
feeding the earth with what they let go.
We never rake them. The earth heals itself.
We never cut its hair, and its soil grows strong
among weeds and grass, burrs and cotton tree seed.
In April we are ready to begin anew, rain
or no rain, cruel month or time of satisfaction.
The perennials arrive first, lifting their heads,
lilies and pampas, a rose that is not a rose
but wishes to be one, nightshades and tulips.
Trees blossom in purples and magentas,
pinks and reds, flamboyant and bold.
We weed weeds and select weeds we will nurture.
Near the back fence the dandelion prosper
ready to harvest their leaves for greens
and a Native American flour for fry bread.
Nearby we settle on a bench in our Zen zone
a shallow muddy pond for water lilies and frogs,
peepers and mud puppies. We do not cut
the grass where the thorns grow heavy
and every year a family of voles visits with us.

Our garden erupts into one rainbow or another—
a shiny blue early May, white chocolate blossoms
at the start of June, long wings of spider plant whites
and every shade of green into July and August.
We harvest mulberries and cherries, wild grape leaves,
mushrooms and edible petals bright red and pink.
When October arrives, we are almost done,
there being little left to do but let autumn take over,
let the grasses go to browns and maroons, oranges
and soft pastels. We put everything away for the season
and ask each other when will enough ever be enough.
Enough never is enough. We begin the planning for spring.

Club Gluttony

Ruth Z. Deming

We meet in the back room
of the Galaxy Café. Candles
light our tables and we
begin each Monday with
a prayer. Please, God,
or Whomever, help us find
food foul, tasteless
or reminding us of rats
and their long tails.
Lovable potbellied Tommy
was found dead in his bed.

Cyberfood

Roberta Gould

You have eaten completely
every dish on the virtual screen
Nothing's lacking! Satisfaction
is your state. It's easy!
You just sit there
receive a menu and choose
Then you're full.
Freedom is great!

With only a click
what you want becomes yours
(How long will it last?
Will you need to eat later?)
Too much thought! Put your mind
on another image. Have faith
and you'll never go hungry

Gluttony

Howard Brown

As Mae West said: *"Too much
of a good thing is wonderful."* And
though she seems to have spoken
in jest, she could well have been
serious, I suppose.

For in this world, where unbridled
consumption is the order of the day,
you can find any number of
fellow travelers who'll gladly
accompany you down this road.

Still, in death, only three entrees
are said to appear on the menus
of the intemperate; those delicacies
being rats, snakes and, if my memory
serves me correctly, the common toad!

Remember too, trencherman, the patron saint of gluttons is Beelzebub, Lord of the Flies, a very nasty fellow, who in Hell ranks second only to the Devil himself.

So, gourmand, take note: It's a very short step from the measured moderation of Epicurus to the outrageous excesses of our friend, Mr. Creosote.

Thin Lines

Rikki Santer

Either way, with thick paws or bony digits it's crammed in mouth.
    There's a thin line between corpulence and hunger
    that thin line between sucked caviar from fingernails or sucked
    from a paper straw a half-pint carton of charity milk
    that thin line between dented cans of three-bean salad
    and Venezuelan Porcelana Criollo beans
    for a $750 chocolate cupcake at the Palazzo in Vegas
    the context of appetite stirs the pot

A thin line between raw and cooked
    brick-a-brackery of what follows that first ember
    the clotted and emulsified
    the shredded and sheared
    her jarred peaches and the shelved ghosts that leave
    another raw

A thin line between boiled and baked
    the table a frothy sea in the chemistry of best intentions
    what dies twice from hard white bone
    too linear is what happens without sauce
    but burned beans make no apologies

A thin line between sweet and sour
    the barbecued tang of terror under rack
    of ribs that resemble yours
    a fortune cookie with news to regret
    congregation of bruised apples in the throes
    of maraschino conversion
    to learn sweetness is to learn sour first

There is a thin line between fresh and stale
    when the sauerkraut of a marriage that began
    gleaming with ghee
    turns knell for a rancid spreadable
    when at a bus stop a three-legged squirrel
    forages for crumbs where last night
    same bench
    neighborhood boy
    drive-by shooting

Chi (Eat): Insight into Chinese Civilization

Changming Yuan

They are a big-stomached nation:

Their subtlest art is cuisine
Their most developed industry is food processing
Their typical greeting is: have you *eaten* yet?
Their most significant social gathering is a dinner party
Their happiest moment is when they enjoy foods
Their last thing to do upon death is to eat what they've always wanted
Their most prosperous business is restauranting
Their best place for decision making is around a dinner table
Their most courageous thing to do is to be the first to taste something
Their most advanced knowledge is about whatever is edible.
Their proudest experience is they have eaten something
               you cannot even imagine
Their key word in describing a social event or interaction is *eating*

     Of all ethnic groups in the human world
    In every corner of a populated place in this planet
  They are most creative, most adventurous, most attentive,
                 most passionate
Most efficient, most quality-minded, most aesthetic, most civilized
             Whenever it comes to *chi*

Lucky to Be Here

Jon Bennett

I was coming off Oxycontin
in a room full of
some really waspy friends.
"This foie gras is crap," I said.
One of them pointed a finger,
"You're lucky to be here!" she said.
I didn't feel lucky.
I felt bored.
These days I'm in
different rooms
in the slum with bums
but passing the basket I say
"I'm lucky to be here,"
and I mean it.

Saving Lives

Carolyn Cordon

Gluttony would never be my sin
My needs for food are scant
Quality preferred over quantity
The little that lasts for long

I value my health, look after self,
Vegetables and fruit my friends
Carrots over banana's delights
Savoury over sweet ...

Food's not a vice to bring me down
I dine with decorous nibbles
No shoving food down in hasty gulps
That's not the way I go

Looking at vices, sloth, that's mine
Not proud of that, but there's worse
Sitting and thinking, I call it
But that isn't really the truth

I'm a poet, words will light my fuse
Line produced after thoughtful line
Does anyone else know or care?
Do my words save people's lives?

Actually yes, I think they can
I've connected to others at times
Poetry written at a slothful rate
Or lines scribbled out in haste

Connection helps healing happen,
Knowing you're not alone
Not weird, unwanted, anymore,
When another understands ...

Fat City

Louise Hofmeister

When she drove down Main
for the third time
she finally grasped
the sights and signs.

"The Ruby River
Steak house"
Really?

The "Ho-hum Hotel"
next door to
the "Best Bet Inn" –
Both seemed like
shaky guarantees.

Then the buffet
billboards boosting
dirt-cheap smorgasbords
"All you can eat!"
on every block

Hardly like her hometown
where "Yoga class!"
and "Kale salad!"
shout out from
chalk paint storefronts.

Sure, as expected
there were neon "Girls"
quite broadly represented

But once you got
past that,
and once you'd
gambled all your cash,

did you come to the place
where happiness
lives in a bottomless
basket of bread?

Kummerspeck
or Grief Bacon (with thanks to the Germans)

Marian Urquilla

there is a word
for the weight you put on
when fear
displaces order
stretching empty places
into spirals of
longing

for before diagnosis
for before pain
for before cutting
for before coughing
for before falling
for before any signal
for before any knowing

there is a word
for embalming yourself
with salty mouth
and burned fingers
for holding yourself
inside a tide of undone time
emptied of restraint
because your mouth is
screaming no
and the only
thing left
is to
fill it
fill it
fill it
swallow
swallow
swallow

Forbidden Fruit

Joanne Rizzo

I will eat with my hands
she said
not challenge or threat
a fact

I stand and watch

she swallows morsel
after bit
crimson juice of plump berries
trickles vines down her arms
stains seductive blossoms of her lips

my arms hang primly at my sides
I dutifully chew
and swallow
measured portions
nutritional combinations
chosen thoughtfully for me
specifically selected to be eaten
neatly
completely
leaving no trace of juice
or pulp
or crumb

the sharp tine of fork
pricks my tongue
I do not bleed

she selects each bit deliberately
a queen picking through
her treasure
a pause
a thought
to choose the perfect jewel

she places a succulent slice
of pear
on her gladdened tongue
eyes closed
face a picture of desire
and
one
  by
    one
slowly
licks
each finger

saliva burns my mouth

I carefully lean toward her
the scent
of satisfaction
lingers
on her breath

Oblivious

Marcia Conover

Out of bed brush the teeth grab a cupcake
There's Facebook to read, cup of coffee
to get the blood flowing. Ooh that went quick
time to fry some bacon and a couple of eggs.
It's so important to eat some protein at the beginning of the day.
One, no two .... well six slices should be ok.
A glass of milk and orange juice on the side
washing down every single bite.
Bread in the toaster smells divine.
It will taste better with butter
plus two or three spoons of strawberry jam.
Breakfast is finished and time to get dressed.
I swear these pants have shrunk a 1/2 size at best.
Opening the pantry to make a list.
The things that are needed to refill the fridge.
Swiss cake rolls, whipped cream and hot dogs.
The freezer is empty as well, we need
Two cartons of ice cream, four frozen pies.
Restocking this house with foods to survive.
After all that hard work the stomach
is growling it's time for a snack.

Grabbing a bag of chips, animal crackers and
two sodas a bit of a thirst to quench.
The time oh my it's already 9:30.
Got to start planning lunch better hurry.
Since the shelves are getting empty
I'll get Lunch out on the go.
Two double, no triple cheeseburgers,
fries on the side, super size those please.
Add a sweet tea without all the ice.
Twenty five minutes from start to finish.
No time to waste when you're in a hurry
On to the grocery store to fulfill the list.
Scurrying down each aisle adding items.
Some not needed but look delish.
Ah a large sack of chocolate bars
for a snack in the car.
Where has the day gone and those
chocolate snacks? I must have bought
a bag just half full. Now it's empty
where it lies on the floor.
Yes a glass of wine is in order as I decide,
what shall be for dinner and how many sides?
Remembering a meeting I must attend ....
I guess we'll just order a couple of pizzas instead.

Breadsticks with cheese sauce let's get the works.
My mouth is watering as I spit out the words.
Back from the meeting where there were desserts.
Homemade brownies and cookies and goods.
The TV is on and a movie is playing.
The Family has gathered in their favorite seats.
Things are in hands: ice cream, candy,
Sodas, bags of chips and other treats.
My stomach is bigger than my eyes that's for sure.
I'll just sit for a while and share all these sweets
Then a thought crossed my mind
as I sat there and watched.
Maybe I should join the gym ......
What? Are you serious? The echos rang out.
You're a glutton for punishment please leave us out.
Well that's the last thing I want to be.
A "glutton" I wouldn't use that word to describe me.

I like you for the way fruit pops in your mouth.

Linda Kohler

I love you for so many reasons
but I am fascinated with watching you
eat fruit,
the way you get greedy with grapes
even if there are not enough left for me:

the only time you forget consideration.

I like how your hunger overtakes you,
the way you split skin,
pluck more while you're still chewing.

I like your art, your hands, your face,
your heart

but the thrill of watching you devour fruit
is, to my eyes, vitamins.

You know it is too much for me
when I grab you and suck the pulp
from your mouth, you see,

your appetite overtakes me too.

Teacups, Teacups— Everywhere ... and Not a Scone in Sight

Shawn Aveningo Sanders

So many dishes, yet so little food
her teacups runneth over with —

                                      { air }

She's ready for a perpetual tea party
in every room of the house.

Be her guest.
Each surface set:
kitchen counter, coffee table, desk, dinette,
bed trays, vanity, bookshelves, patio set.

A collection of teapots, teacups & saucers
that would put the Mad Hatter to shame:

Fine Bone in *Wedgwood, Spode, Royal Doulton,
Waterford, Lenox, Villeroy & Boch,
Noritake, Mikasa,* and *Dansk—*

Depression Glass in *Princess, Cherry Blossom,*
Ruby Red, Moonbeam, and even *Shirley Temple*—

Thrift store finds and souvenir-shop treasures
of a lifetime.

And the doilies!
Good God, those doilies!

And yet when I visit:
"I hear there's a new tea room across town,
cucumber canapés to simply die for.
Shall we go out for a bite?"

Sure Mom,
no sense having dishes to wash
after we gorge ourselves on finger foods
and chamomile.

          Now to choose a proper chapeau . . .

Fat Ronald Cheats

Ron Lavalette

All the ads say it's hot and juicy,
and it's hot alright, but the juicy's
really just grease that congeals
pretty quickly back into fat. He's
reasonably sure he can feel it
coating his cluttered arteries
even before he swallows.
None of this, though,
keeps him from eating there
four or five times a week,
nor does he ever—even remotely—
consider ordering a drive-thru salad
or the lo-cal fruit parfait.

His wife says he's turning into a
bacon-wrapped double cheeseburger,
but all he hears is how delicious he is,
how much she wants to gobble him up.
He still loves her madly, but she
just doesn't satisfy him anymore.
He's always somewhat disappointed
when even her tastiest dishes
refuse to dribble down his chin,
promise neither cardiac arrhythmia
nor the ever-expanding waistline
he's come to honor and obey.

Feast or Fast

Mark Hudson

I was a life-long glutton. I blame
it on ten years working in the restaurant
industry.

One of the jobs I held senior
year in high school was in a mental
hospital kitchen, as a dishwasher.
I started out working the counter.
The first day I was there, nobody
was around, so I grabbed some
spaghetti, and twirled it in the
air, and held it to my lips.
 Just then a nurse walked
in and saw me. She said, "I'm
going to report you, that's not
sanitary!" But she never did.
Then I saw a lady in the back
drop a cookie on the floor, and
put it back on the tray.

Then my boss yelled
at me, because I accidentally
sent a bunch of cake to the
diabetic wing. I probably

didn't know the difference
at the time, and now, I
have diabetes!

    Then, that summer
of 1989, I went with my uncle
to stay on Martha's Vineyard,
Massachusetts, and I needed
to get a job, so I got a job
at the best Italian restaurant
on the island. When I applied
for the job, the manager said,
"Would you like to work
full-time, or part-time?"
And I said, "Fart-time,"
which is probably what
I was doing, after eating
free Italian food!

    I washed dishes,
and every time they burned
some food, they'd say,
"Give it to the dishwasher."
    I think that's when
I started to get fat!

    Then I got a job back home,
where I worked in a movie
theater, making butter-flavored
popcorn. I ate a lot of it, and
blew up like a balloon.

There were three restaurants
to eat there, Munch-a-Bunch,
owned by a Korean man, with
a cardboard picture of a cow,
Mustard's Last Stand, a hot dog
and hamburger place, and a
Chinese restaurant that nobody
went to but me, and they used
to say, "You're single-handedly
keeping them in business."
I would get white rice, and
put butter flavored goo on it,
and my manager would come
out and say, "What do you
want to give yourself, a cardiac
arrest?' On top of all that, I
was a chain smoker!

    There was a man at
Mustard's who nicknamed
me "Psycho" and some
of the workers at the theater
thought I was a psycho, too.
I got a second job in a
warehouse making misting
systems for grocery stores,
and a girl at the movie theater job
told her boyfriend, "That psycho
guy has a new job making missile
systems!"

At the warehouse, we'd
eat out on Friday, and bring
food back to the warehouse.
We'd go to this place called
"Munch-times," and my
supervisor would joke,
"You can eat Munch-times
with your booty-stained hands."
Because I'd start out the day
with a pitcher of coffee, and
then sit on the toilet when I
was supposed to be working.

The Korean man at
Munch-a-Bunch would always
be teasing me because I was
fat, so I wouldn't eat at his
restaurant, and I'd go to
Mustard's Last Stand, and
I'd walk back bloated, and
he'd be standing there with
his arms crossed, as if he
couldn't understand why
I didn't go to his store!

This very January
I was in the hospital, and
I was diagnosed with diabetes.
Since then, I went from weighing
285 to 212. And I hope to
keep losing weight, and
no longer be a glutton.

Invisible Trenches Between Me And My Other Self

Judah Eli Cricelli

Gamma radiation
But it's two lips instead,
It's the muscles at the sides of
Your mouth.
And when I talk to you
I trip over my words a little,
Because I want to eat this moment.
Reflections and perfect little sections,
Dissident today, and then
Don't start, I hear you say,
I'm here, don't start, I hear you say
Because it doesn't last a day.
I've started eating us away, I type,
And type about the blots
Inside my head, the shoes and socks,

But then, it
Doesn't
Matter:
Anti-matter, and
Lo-fi
Eyes—
What's your number?
Nylon thighs;
The emptiness I left behind
And ethyl acetate,
Faintly grey—
You're at home
You want to
Be alone—
No.
Whirring voices,
Neon snow,
Argon pointless,
Pointless, slow
In slowmo motion
My back against yours
With dogs barking in my blood
And wind howling inside my bones.

Rough surfaces and
Faceless surfaces and
Placeless surfaces
In your art,
With no place for your
Heart,
There's no place for
Your heart and then
There's something I've forgotten
And it doesn't rhyme
With heart,
A part apart from me
You walk to me
And talk into me
Longer and my
Hunger eats me stronger
And my long legs get me farther
From the life that I would rather
But we're strangers together.

Prose

Prose

69	Our Enormous Fat Man	*Steven Gowin*
72	Coming Home	*Sharron Hough*
76	In the Event of a Famine	*Salvatore DiFalco*
79	crap	*Alan C. Baird*
82	The Art Gallery Reception	*Jeffrey Weisman*
84	Boys and Their Potatoes	*Rob Walton*
86	Saturday Night Gluttony	*Bryan Jansing*
89	Hi, My Name Is Dorothy, and I'm a Sugar Addict *Dorothy Rice*	
93	The Blue	*Andrew Grenfell*
96	The Binge Catering Service	*Edward Ahern*
100	Pigswill	*Tracy Lee-Newman*
102	The Means	*Cynthia Leslie-Bole*
105	Edward takes his picnic on the bus	*Sarah Salway*
108	Just Silly Things I Do with Food	*Noah Grabeel*
111	Local BBQ	*Jemshed Khan*
112	Folie à Deux	*Iris N. Schwartz*
115	Flying	*Townsend Walker*
116	Chain of Events	*Mark Budman*
119	The Big Lunch	*Elaine Barnard*
123	Food for Thought	*Larry Lefkowitz*
127	Eater in the Woods	*John Kujawski*

130	Candy *Jake Greenblot*	
132	The League of the Loved *Peter Lingard*	
137	Gentlemen in Waiting *Tom Fegan*	
141	The Recent History of the Sánchez Family Tragedies: Part II *Guilie Castillo Oriard*	
145	Frosting by the Forkful *Andrea Diede*	
148	Eaten *Steven Carr*	
152	The Return of Red Ledbetter Episode 2 *JP Lundstrom*	
157	Cashew Nuts *Nod Ghosh*	
162	Another Kind of Surprise Party *Paul Beckman*	
165	The Full Platter *Abha Iyengar*	
167	Gluttony *Michael Webb*	
170	You Gonna Eat That? *Wayne Scheer*	

Our Enormous Fat Man

Steven Gowin

How did we get so hard, and beyond that, mean? Dad didn't know. Neither did I. We'd no history of it, no record.

Hully Palmer, at 390 pounds, could barely walk and slept nights upright, painfully and without peace, in his Dodge Power Wagon. Lying prone would have crushed his heart, would have killed him.

Oleaginous folds, arm and belly and thigh, fat over fat, always wet, chapped red, burning with itch, vexed him constantly. His face glowed bright red, blood pushing hard on his arteries, blood too close to the skin's surface.

Pity would have been appropriate. Yet, townsfolk whispered behind his back. Shouldn't he do something about it. So lazy. A gluttonous swine. Hadn't his mother kept him too long at tit, breast feeding 'til four? Look. Look at him now. A fat man. Our enormous fat man.

We savored the idea of Hully as something inferior, someone who must remain other, lesser, a perverse measure of our own worth. Surely no mirror could reflect the disgust of the whole, no bouquet mask the pervasive reek of adiposity.

Dad, more charitable, blamed the big man's glands. It wasn't Hully's fault. Besides, hadn't Hully taken in Mike Harmon's mangy dog Gloria, when Mike passed away? Nobody else had done. Yup. Glands run amok.

When the end came, most of us cared about Hully's death only insofar as we'd miss reviling him. But that didn't seem right, and Dad agreed. He said I should find out what had happened, get the facts, record the accident. So, I did.

I asked the redneck Basset brothers, and I questioned the Palmer and Stump cousins. I talked to Ladies' Aid ladies and the volunteer firemen who'd been there. Unversed in subterfuge and convinced of their innocence, they all talked.

It began South of town in a shallow valley below corn and soybean fields at Madison Pond. A victim of modern agriculture, fertilizer runoff had transformed the spot into a three-acre scum hole, a fetid verdant cancer, an infection.

Our community, too cheap for a cleanup, nevertheless met there yearly for an August picnic of undercooked barbecued pork, fatty hamburger, hot mayonnaise-heavy salads, and beer drinking to excess.

Hully'd arrived at noon and pulled the Power Wagon into the weeds near the picnic tables the better to hear our endless back biting. Someone brought him a bright pink hot dog and a runny jello-cream dish. He'd left them on the dash, untouched, before falling asleep.

About two in the afternoon though, as the sun beat hard, Hully, now drenched in sweat, got himself up and out of that hot pickup cab, rolled up his pant legs, pried off his shoes, and toddled off on tiny ivory feet toward the Madison Pond dock.

Halfway to the end of that rickety pier, still the gargantuan baby, he'd dropped to hands and knees, and splintering his palms as he went, crawled to dock's edge.

There, he'd pushed himself up from the elbows to peer into a break in the scum. And twisting his crimson head side to side to side, he was able to behold his own greasy reflection.

When the pier creaked, and crackled and gave way, Hully Palmer followed it down, down, into five feet of slimy glop.

Face under water now, he did flounder hilariously, flapping his arms, fighting for breath above the muck.

Most of the picnickers simply stood by laughing at this new comedy, but as Hully's struggle subsided, they began wondering if all was well. Finally, Hully's cousin, Ike Palmer, inebriated and hooting, stumbled into the scum to rescue the big boy.

But with the mud that sucked at the drunkard's heels and the victim's enormity, Ike could not budge Hully. Four volunteer firemen finally waded in and dragged Hully out. But whether from drowning or heart failure (no one believed in autopsy), Hully'd perished in the water.

So as not to address our own shortcomings, neglect, and chosen lack of compassion, we now only dimly acknowledge Hully Palmer or any complicity in his death. And in a few years, most here will have forgotten our enormous fat man completely.

But Dad and I remember. We know the story. We talked about it. We got it down.

Coming Home

Sharron Hough

Pinpointing where it started was one thing, containing it was something entirely different. In the time it took to construct walls around Ward Four in Simbal Camp, the outbreak had spread to all five wards. This was the biggest epidemic the camp had seen in years. Nothing noteworthy had hit the news from this part of Jammu since the stabbing in 2016, but this was catastrophic.

Word of the outbreak first came from the primary health centre within the camp. In plague proportions, people were experiencing severe flu-like symptoms accompanied by skin eruptions and alopecia. It was when the sickness escalated to high fever and, soon after, death, that the World Health Organisation was called in. They couldn't deploy their teams quickly enough.

When Dameer Sadid stepped off the plane at Jammu Airport, his expectations, he thought, were realistic. It had been several years since he'd been back to India after graduating medical school and completing his internship at SMHS Hospital in Kashmir. He'd applied for a position with WHO just as his internship was ending and was accepted, where he was immediately transferred to Sierra Leone to help manage the Ebola outbreak, which at the time had been declared the 'most severe acute public health emergency seen in modern times.' He had seen the worst and treated the worst.

Drenched with sweat in the humid Indian heat, the WHO team was quickly escorted to an Ashok painted and tarped in military khaki. The small amount of equipment that came with them was loaded into the back of the truck. It wasn't much, but it was enough to start preliminary tests to see what they were up against.

Taking the RS Pura Road out of the airport, their first stop was the Niranjan Hospital where they were scheduled for a complete briefing. It was only then they understood the full extent of the situation. Full body Hazchem equipment was going to be needed, and if they came out alive, quarantine of at least six months would be waiting for them on the other side. But nothing could prepare them for the magnitude of the situation as they headed back out on the road to Simbal.

Twenty minutes down the road and the truck slowed to a stop. Dameer stood, craning his neck to see around the back of the truck when the driver appeared.

"I just got word from Niranjan Hospital. They said not to bother with Simbal Camp, but start work in Hakal. It has already spread that far."

"We still need to get up there to help the survivors and dispose of the dead. We can't just let them rot, it will cause more disease, especially if it gets to the Tawi River."

"We can't go any further, sir. The military has been called in and will be dropping incendiary devices on the entire camp."

"They can't! What of the survivors?"

"I'm sorry, sir, the order has been given and I cannot take the risk. We have been told to keep clear and stay in Hakal."

The truck jolted and jostled as it veered off the road into the scrub to get around the barrier at Sambal Road. The military was already evacuating Dinde Kalan, the line of exiting traffic stretching like a python of army green. As they approached Hakal, they were stopped at another barricade but were quickly ushered through.

"This does not look good," Dameer said.

It was the smell that hit them first. The entire team put on full-face respirators in an attempt not to gag. Donning their gloves and sealing them into the cuffs of their protective overalls, they checked each other for gaps in their gear.

They planned to get to the nearest health centre and set up a station where samples could be taken and patients could be monitored. Once they knew the incubation period and how it was spreading, they would know how to contain the outbreak.

As the team stepped out of the truck, hefting bags of equipment on their shoulders, a dark cloud circled above them. Thousands of birds of prey swirled the sky like a feathered whirlpool, as one by one they descended to the ground.

Nothing could have prepared Dameer and his team for the sight before them. Piles of bodies, spilling out of homes, shops and buildings, frozen in rictus as if stepping into the fresh air meant instant death.

Smothering the bodies like lice were the vultures, ripping and tearing at the flesh of the deceased, their feathers glistening as they bathed in the blood of their gluttony. The urgency with which they ate was unnatural. Gorging themselves as though they had been starved, only to vomit, turn back and start to feed again in the same frantic delirium.

Dameer turned at the sound of the driver spraying a fountain of what was once his lunch beside the truck. Thinking it a natural reaction to such a horrific sight, he moved to help fix the poor man's respirator back around his face. Then he noticed his skin. It had already started to blister and ooze. He was infected.

"We have to get out of here!" Dameer shouted. "There is nothing we can do. You saw how quickly it affected him. It's changing. There's zero incubation period."

As the team clambered back into the truck, Dameer opened his backpack and grabbed a hypodermic needle. He didn't have time to attach a vial; a syringe full was all he could take. He stabbed the needle into the driver's carotid and drew back the plunger.

"No time! Get in the truck!" the new designated driver shouted. Turning the truck around, he floored it, just as fighter jets roared above the circling spiral of scavengers.

Dameer carefully tried to recap the needle, one of the first things they were told never to do in training. As the truck jostled and swerved along the road, the needle missed its mark, piercing his glove. He could see the blood well beneath the latex. Fire spread up his arm like acid, corroding him from the inside, his skin bubbling as it burnt. He fumbled at his respirator, trying to add reinforcement for what was to come, but he was too late. Nothing could stop what his stomach violently delivered, as the airline's vegetarian option burst from the seals and splattered across the dash.

In the Event of a Famine

Salvatore DiFalco

"Everything in this house is edible," said the real estate agent. "I mean everything, the foundation, the plaster, the windows. That is to say, in the event of a famine, a family of three would be able to survive for approximately three years eating the house."

I studied the dark-hued foyer. My wife checked out a bouquet of red roses in a glass vase resting on a handkerchief table against a wall.

The real estate agent, whose sideburns looked like they had not matriculated from the late twentieth century, smiled. "You wondering how all this is edible," he said.

My wife looked at me with knitted brows. I did not know if this expressed healthy skepticism or anger that I had brought her to this unusual house.

"All the hardwood, floorboards, moldings, and window frames are made of a material akin to power bars, chockfull of amino acids and antioxidants." He walked over to the handkerchief table and picked up the vase with the roses. "This vase is made of spun sugar and gelatin, perhaps not the most nutritious material, but tasty in a pinch. And the roses—" He pulled one out of the vase and chomped it. "Delicious. Actually made from kale, beets and sea salt, believe it or not."

"They've thought of everything," I said.

My wife sniffed and looked up at the light fixture.

"Yes, that too is edible," said the real estate agent. "Made from soybeans."

I felt my elbow being tugged. My wife wanted a word with me in private.

"Give us a moment," I said.

"By all means."

"Honey, what is it?"

My wife shook her head. "Like, are we expecting a famine soon?"

"Sweetie, you just never know. The world economy is on the brink of collapse."

"It's always on the brink."

"That's what I'm saying. One of these days the shit's gonna hit the fan."

"It is a lovely house."

I asked the real estate agent about durability.

"Well, if you don't start nibbling—and that's been a problem with some folks—if you don't start, you know, breaking off little pieces here and there, and weakening the structure, hell, it will last as long as any house. They've really put the science into this."

"You mean to say people start nibbling at it?" my wife said.

The real estate agent chuckled. "You'd be amazed. That's the single biggest problem with these houses. People start eating them."

"That's messed up," I said, feeling superior. "Why would people start eating their own house if they didn't have to?"

"Let me put it this way," said the real estate agent. He stepped to the wall where a framed portrait of a brown horse hung, unimpressive as artworks go. He removed the portrait from the wall and brought it to us. "Break off a piece," he said.

"What?" I said.

"No, really. Break off a piece."

I broke off a piece of the frame. He told me to try it. I stared at it for a moment before I brought the brown chunk to my teeth. I bit in and it crumbled to pressure. Sweet and brittle. It tasted like peanut brittle.

"It is peanut brittle," said the real estate agent, urging my wife to try some.

It was buttery and delicious, the roasted peanuts exploding with flavour. Probably the best peanut brittle I had ever tasted. I couldn't believe how good it was. My wife broke off a chunk and bit into it. Her eyes popped open.

"I know," I said, acknowledging her delight and surprise.

The real estate agent smiled mirthlessly. "Yeah, that's a problem. They made the materials too good, too tasty."

"People lack self-control," I said, smacking my lips and eating more of the amazing peanut brittle.

"Yeah," he said, "that's exactly right. They should have probably made it out of less palatable materials—one project strictly used seaweed, but proved to be useless after excessive rainfall." He looked at the horse in the portrait as though appraising its aesthetic value. "Folks, I'm gonna be straight with you. You need to be on your best behaviour if you want this house to work. Not everyone's cut out for it."

My wife's eyes fluttered as she finished the chunk of frame. I know she wanted more, but the real estate agent didn't offer more. Instead he broke off a chunk of the portrait and started eating it himself, his eyes half shut.

crap

Alan C. Baird

So you sit there, wondering why you ate those huge blocks of cheese during the past couple of days, feeling like you're carrying around an anvil inside your butt, and nothing will ever come out, ever again, so you resign yourself to standing up, unsuccessful for the thirty-fourth time, when you hear that gurgling sound in the pit of your stomach, and YES, it may just happen right now, so you bear down, grunting and groaning, and your face turns bright purple-red, and you imagine that you're gonna have a stroke, right there on the toilet, so the headlines will read 'Man's Head Explodes While He Takes A Dump', and your friends will make fun of you at the funeral, pointing and laughing at your casket, blowing fart noises on the backs of their hands, and you will lie there ashamed in your coffin, turning as bright purple-red as you are right now, still grunting and groaning, still trying to get rid of the butt-anvil so your pallbearers' spines won't snap like twigs when they hoist you up onto their shoulders, and then you feel like your sphincter is gonna rip right open, the obstetrician saying, "You're eight centimeters dilated, things are going well," and you fly into a rage because that effete cocksucker is calling out measurements that no real flag-waving God-fearing Murrican could ever understand, so why the fuck doesn't he convert metric into inches and feet and friggin' YARDS, or at least fingers, like "You're three fingers dilated, now four, and now I can slide my fist into your ass, so you'll never be heterosexual again," and your friends will call you "queer," and your face will turn purple-red from shame, almost as bright as it is right now, and you can feel the cork turd crowning, holy shit, there must be massive ripping and tearing, 'coz the butt-anvil is coming out sideways, and you beg the obstetrician to go ahead and make you light-in-the-loafers by reaching WAY up inside and turning that motherfucker around so your ass won't be quite so disfigured, hell, you had a cute virginal ass at one point in your life, before you started gobbling down all that cheese six months ago, and the butt-anvil is spreading your cheeks so wide that you'll never be able to fit into a standard-size airline seat again, they'll force you to buy two seats like that enormously fat guy on the cable channel who can't fit through his front door because he's so damn chubby, and you wonder if you'll ever be able to fit back through your own bathroom door, the situation seemed so innocent when you walked in, eight hours ago, to make your eighty-seventh attempt to get rid of the anvil that's been forming a butt-plug in your colon since you started eating all that cheese fifteen years ago, and you sit there with your chin resting on the back of your hand, like that sculpture by Rodin, wondering if the great man ever looked at his own handiwork and sniffed a faint whiff of farts and turds and liquid diarrhea, oh for the lovely release of a watery squirt right now, you remember that picture of the kid who had a bad case of the explosive runs, so he stood on top of a block of granite, bent over, dropped trou and had his friend take a snapshot of the powerful geyser-like brown blast that shot out of his ass, and you think, you ponder, you meditate like Rodin, and you fantasize about being frozen in this position, so the local newspaper takes a photo for their Weird Shit section, 'Man Who Became Statue While Attempting To Push Out Gigantic Butt-Anvil', but you don't know if you have the courage to keep squeezing, pumping and grunting, so you pray to the Greater Butt Intelligence Of The Universe, saying, "Please deliver me from this impasse, I am at a crossroads, and I will never again question the holy goodness of your laxative-like presence, if only you will have mercy on me in this, my hour of need, I promise to sing your praises to all my friends, and make them so bored that they will begin to avoid me and my Born-Again Butt fervor," and then a white light descends upon you and you feel a pain in your no-longer-cherry ass that is more intense than any pain you have ever felt, and you begin to wonder if it might be toaster-in-the-tub time, but you retreat from the awful specter of self-annihilation by breathing deep and fast, panting breaths, and you squeal like a stuck pig, and you hear a tiny splash in the toilet water, and you moan your gratitude and you feel a warm relief spreading through your soul like you will never-ever-ever feel again in your entire life even if you live to be a hundred and fifty, and you look down to see that the product of all this pain and sweat and monumental effort is only the size of a small marble, and you realize that you'll be forced to go back to the beginning and start all over again.

Shit.

The Art Gallery Reception

Jeffrey Weisman

Few people look at the art at art openings. They seem to regard the art gallery opening as a social event. "Let's get together at the Bernoulli Gallery; then we'll go to dinner."

Free food, even less than sophisticated hors d'oeuvres, draws a cohort of gluttons. Their presence reminds me of the figures in a Ferdinand Botero painting. Remember the Woody Allen line, "The food was lousy and the portions were small."

Gallery openings, no matter where, seem to attract these *schnorrers*. (This Yiddish expression describes a glutton who attempts to give the impression of respectability. This seems to fit in with an art gallery.)

What can a gallery owner or curator do to motivate more people to look at the art? How can they get the gluttons to leave the food for a moment? Isn't that the reason for the opening, the first step toward a purchase or investment?

Perhaps the gallery manager can hang images of food – a painting, a print, a photograph – unrelated to the gallery show. In the program for the opening that lists the art, it can pose questions whose answers require looking at the art.

Which painting has a cake or peach or rutabaga? Which photograph shows the manicotti, etc.?

Make it fun. Offer a prize for the correct answer(s), perhaps a left-over fruit cake. By making people, gluttons included, look more closely at the art and the title/price cards, interest will increase. Plus the gallery will record the attendees' contact information beyond a random sign-in book.

Gluttons will always attend art gallery openings. Free food the draw. Getting them away from the food, albeit momentarily, in an enticing manner just might work.

Boys and Their Potatoes

Rob Walton

"All right, Ben? What you up to?"

"New recipe."

"Right. That looks like a sack of potatoes."

"Early days, mate. Early days. Watch this."

Yusuf watched Ben peel potatoes for an hour. Then he watched him cut some and chip some and bake some and mash some and put some in pans and some in the oven. There was a pile of unnaturally large potatoes which remained on the side of the bench. Yusuf didn't have that many friends or interests, so he told himself he'd wait for another hour to see how things panned out. Then he laughed to himself.

"I'm trying to cook here, mate. I can't concentrate if you're laughing. What's so funny?"

"Nothing. I mean, I just said 'panned out' in my head and it tickled me. So what's this all about, then?"

"You've heard about them chefs who put a pigeon inside a duck inside a chicken inside a turkey?"

"No."

"Well, I'm doing the same sort of thing, only with potatoes. I'm baking these massive potatoes, and then filling the skins. I put a fondant potato in the middle, stack chipped potatoes and wedges around it and then spoon a load of creamed potatoes over the top. With a few regular boiled potatoes. I mustn't forget them."

"Right. I see." Yusuf paused. "And then what?"

"And then, my mate, we eat the lot."

"Good. That's really good, is that. Just one thing."

"Yes, mate?"

"Can I have potato salad with it?"

Saturday Night Gluttony

Bryan Jansing

"You know why they call themselves Phish, right?" I say to Ace.

"No," he says, "Why?"

"Cause they stink."

The heavyset doorman, a Chicago brother in a fedora hat, eyeballs us through the crowded restaurant. The on- and off-duty cops give us glances. Fat Bastard smooths it over because he's the only sober one and he has presence. We shouldn't be allowed in public. But they let us in.

We sit at a very large table at Pete's Kitchen on the covered veranda as Saturday's crowd distils into the late night. They are drunk and nourished and now they're going home to sleep off the booze we've fed them all night, while the eight of us sit down to have dinner. We too are in a Saturday night state. We reek of booze, some of the stink from our clothes. Even though it is dying down, our waitress hustles.

"What can I get for you to drink?"

We all order coffees.

"I'll have a milkshake," Fat Bastard says. "I'll also have an iced tea."

The waitress begins to step away.

"And a chocolate milk." He sets down the little plastic creamer container along with the other four he's emptied, "And also a cinnamon bun."

They have the best cinnamon buns in the state.

Fat Bastard says, "You dumb asses are gonna follow Phish around." Then he mockingly says in a girly voice, "Ooooh, look at me, I'm following Phish."

We all laugh. Fat Bastard is a large man, a jovial fat guy, very bright, very smart, a Texan through and through whose education has diluted his accent. He's only 29 years old, but he carries himself like a middle-aged businessman. He's been in the business of craft beer from the ground up, along with his brothers King and Porn Star. And while King's main job is the beers that have to fill 69 taps, and Porn Star manages the day-to-day business of running a bar, Fat Bastard is in charge and overseer of all.

He's a cynical son of a bitch with an I-don't-give-a-shit style all of his own. If he had a moto, it would be 'Fuck you. I've got enough friends.'

We all take a dig from Fat Bastard's cinnamon bun so he's ordered another. "I'll have the three egg breakfast," he begins, "with an extra egg, scrambled with sausage and white toast; a side of sausage gravy and a side of extra bacon. I'll have the short stack," he ends, "and another milkshake."

"Damn." I say. "*I'll have a side of this, a stack of that, another side of this.*"

"What?" Fat Bastard says throwing his arms up and laughing.

The waitress flips the page and takes the rest of our orders.

"I'll have the Pork Chop and eggs, over easy," Tobe says. We all laugh.

"Only someone from Iowa would order the pork chops from Pete's," Ace says.

"I want the chicken schlovaki and eggs," I say, "Can I get that with brown gravy and rye, please?"

"Rye?!" Fat Bastard bursts out, "Who the fuck orders schlovaki and eggs and rye bread?"

"And brown gravy?" Pitbull chimes in.

"I'll have one egg," Red says. Red's got long, red, thin hair, very pale skin, large blue eyes on a very slender, pale face. He's tall and lanky, soft-spoken and always wears black; a vampire who is Kay's roommate and old childhood friend from Richmond, VA. "I'll also have," he continues in his Virginia accent, "two slices of bacon…."

I can't help myself. I mimic the Count from Sesame Street, "I'll have, One, hahaha, one egg; two, hahaha, two slices of bacon; and three, yes, thrreee pieces of toast, hahahaha."

The entire table falls over themselves in a roar of laughter.

When the food arrives, Pete's has cleared out. We're still high from our food, laughing and carrying on like it were a Thanksgiving dinner. This bunch of misfits, a group of loners all drawn together under this auspicious little craft beer bar.

Hi, My Name Is Dorothy, and I'm a Sugar Addict

Dorothy Rice

"Well, that's a pretty sweet habit," people say, when I tell them I'm hooked on sugar.

It isn't. It's been said that sugar is as addictive as cocaine. And unlike cocaine, it's legal, cheap and plentiful. If you're a user, you don't have a taste of heroin, a little bit of booze or meth. It's no different with sugar. Given the right combination of supply, time and privacy, I will consume every ounce I can lay hands to, and I'll do it fast. Hardly tasting after the first few mouthfuls. Until I make myself sick and descend into a nightmare-ridden digestive stupor.

I can easily gain ten pounds in a month, without pregnancy or a thyroid condition to blame. One six-month dental check-up, I had eleven cavities. The dentist asked if I'd been crunching hard candies in my sleep. I hadn't. But I do sometimes doze with buttery caramels melting in my mouth.

Triggers for sugar-binging abound, but Halloween through New Year's, the sanctioned over-eating season, is the worst. This past year proved epic. I was in a funk, a combination of seasonal affective disorder, empty nest blues, belated mid-life crisis, and, on top of all that, the nightmare of US politics. Compelling reasons to need "a little something to take the edge off" were as close as the morning paper.

My husband, Bob, always buys our annual supply of Halloween candy. I reminded him to pick a kind that wouldn't tempt me.

"Get something gummy or sour," I said.

"Why would I buy that crap?"

"Well, anything but chocolate, *please*."

"Oh, I'm getting chocolate."

"At least hide it," I said. "And not in one of your usual places."

"Oh, come on. A little chocolate every day is good for you."

Bob is one of those people who can eat one piece, then walk away. Incomprehensible.

Two weeks before Halloween, I returned from running errands. His car was in the drive. I looked for him in his office and there they were. Two jumbo sacks of assorted chocolates, in plain sight on his desk. 120 pieces each. 240 mini candy bars in all. I hefted one sack, then the other, probing for holes in the plastic, heart pounding, simultaneously relieved and bereft not to find any.

It was possible he'd just arrived home and hadn't had time to hide the candy. I made a mental note to remind him. But I never did. As we ate dinner, watched TV, did the dishes, I pictured the candy bars in their shiny wrappers, waiting in the dark, sending out their scent, whispering my name.

I wish I craved sex the way I do sweets. Indiscriminate sex has its consequences, but it doesn't rot your teeth, ruin your health or pack on the pounds. Usually.

I'm 64. A nutritionist calculated my weight, measurements and percentage of body fat and blithely informed me that my metabolic age is 85. No sugar-coating those numbers. I am resigned to a wardrobe of black, elastic waist-band trousers and voluminous tunics that provide chin-to-knee coverage.

For days, I resisted those sacks of candy. But the instant I discovered a tiny hole in one—proof that Bob had started the sampling—my resolve crumbled. I selected one each of the four varieties. Settling into my favorite corner of the couch, I prepared to savor them, then get on with my day. But, like a scratch you can't quite reach, they weren't as satisfying as I'd anticipated. The next four went down faster than the first. I returned to the bag again and again, snitching a few each time, telling myself they would be the last.

The last dozen disappeared in a frenzy, fingers in frantic motion, tearing and shoving, crunching and swallowing, my world reduced to the sensations in my mouth, gone too quickly, demanding more, more. My stomach lurched. The couch was littered with twisted wrappers, my pajama top stained with bits of chocolate, slowly melting from the heat of my body.

Stuffed, nauseous, I buried the wrappers in the trash and stretched out on the couch. Crashing hard, I nodded off. Anything I'd hoped to accomplish would have to wait on the digestive process.

The next morning, a devastating migraine hit. I passed the day in my darkened bedroom, promising a god I only thought of at moments like these that I would never eat half a jumbo sack of Halloween candy again.

Yet over the next few days, I finished it off and started on the second bag.

My gluttony last Halloween, and always, ends in sloth. That part's simple biology. Then shame and regret descend, spawning envy and wrath for the self-disciplined and preternaturally slim. Damn them. Pride keeps me at it; I can, I *will*, put whatever I damn well like in my mouth. As for lust and greed, well, food-porn fuels my fantasies. For me, the seven deadly sins are embodied in a candy wrapper. There is no such thing as just one.

Growing up, sugary treats were doled out as rewards and to keep us quiet. They marked milestones and special occasions. If we skinned a knee or lost a friend, we were offered a lollipop. After childhood, the landscape changed, particularly for girls. Our mothers pointed out the twiggy girls we should emulate if we wanted to be popular, to find love. But by adolescence it was too late. Like so many, I was already a closet emotional eater. Sugar was my medicine, one that eased the pain, until it caused it.

If there is a god who conceived these temptations to test us, did she foresee how prevalent they would become—sugar is in virtually all prepared foods—and how pervasive the need to self-medicate, how popular culture would glorify excess? If she can see me eating myself numb, can she forgive me? Can I?

At least I can't be jailed for it. Yet. There is that. And I can detox. Again.

The Blue

Andrew Grenfell

Daniel would say that there are two types of people. Those who try and grab life with both hands, and those who let the world come to them. The first type hunger for all the chaotic majesty of the world and everything that it can give to them, or that they can take. The second admit it piece by piece, that they may make sense of it, fit it into an ordering.

Lea's the first type of person, always has been. Larger than life, in more ways than one.

But you're okay, right? she asks, big blue dress billowing about as we enter.

Well–

You know how it is. Expelled air as she sits down heavily.

He says he wants "breathing space", I explain. Says he feels trapped, frustrated, sometimes wants to smash things. Better all round, better for everyone.

Lea's lips around the rim of the coffee cup, chintzy nail polish, brassy hair. Just when you think you've worked someone out. Says she knows, it took her a long time to understand how someone so beautiful could be so cruel. But then, her longest relationship was what, eight, nine months?

Be okay because I have to be, when there's no-one else.

Stepped off the edge, just like that. Didn't matter how bright the blue sky was. Things I can only think, can't say. But they happened, nevertheless. Thoughts swimming like trapped fish. The way Daniel yelled at me. The silences after.

Clatter of crockery, chairs scraping, traffic noise. Slash of panic, no reason. Even your best friend in the dark, way it's got to be, I suppose.

Should I be angry? Sad? I'm—

You should feel how you feel, she says.

What if you don't know. How you feel, when the ground moves underneath you. Stepping off the edge, blue all around, a blue that would consume all. Still heavy inside. No wonder I can't eat.

Long stare from an infant in a high chair across the café. Incessant babbling of harried mums. Kid on a phone, shutting everything else out, concentrating hard. That'll be Dylan in a few years.

Eggs benny and a pile of sides arrive. Thanks and flash a smile. Lea following him with her hungry eyes, checking out his butt. Can't go back to that.

The fan spins madly above. White paint flakes down the walls. The bare floors clack with the agitations of the waitstaff. This is a house, after all, merely converted. Lea getting plumper every time I see her. *Curvylicious*, she would say.

Saying how she went to an art class, one of those ones where you paint a picture in between quaffing glasses of red wine.

Water at chest height, then just walks forward, drops off, completely submerged, hair waving like weed. Underneath. He's only four years old.

Cut in, gold on yellow garishly spilling on the plate. The shotgun crunch of sourdough toast. Inners of a sliced avocado laid open like the chopped carcass of some poor nocturnal animal. Noisy lycra-clad Sunday morning riders, shovelling in their well-earned Sunday brunches. Colour and guffawing, barrels of light tumbling through the windows.

How calm he was when it happened. How, even though I'm holding his hand, it takes long seconds to realise that of course he can't swim. How he only started crying when Daniel started shouting at me, but try telling him that–

Another coffee, why not, after all, she says, barely finished the first one.

Nights listening to him breathing, thankful to the universe he's still alive. But still thinking of the silence of an underwater world. With your eyes closed, reaching out with your ears and your arms, your hands… no edge to the blue, a blue that is the first whisper of an infinite darkness.

What do you want out of life if it's not this. Said he didn't know what to do, well that makes two of us, Daniel. And here's me trying to stay calm, finishing ironing his work shirts, bewildered. And what about Dylan, what about our son?

Strong bitter of it curling down into me.

Lea knows something's up, that there's reasons behind reasons, the way she looks at me, even as she forks wilted spinach and sickly Hollandaise into her mouth. There's the doggedness of the glutton in her, the needing to know. But I can't, I can't. I wish we'd sat outside. I wish I didn't feel so tight inside.

I don't want to have everything, the way everyone else seems to want everything. I just want to hold onto what I already have.

The Binge Catering Service

Edward Ahern

The card was double thickness, out-sized, and nubble-surfaced in red foam.

> The Binge Catering Service
> "Anything worth doing is worth doing to excess"
> Miss Manners 203 371 8380

"You need a better pick-up gimmick."

The woman sitting across from me smiled with her mouth but not her eyes. Dark brown, elegantly styled hair, clean-lined, expensive black dress. "No gimmick, Mr. Robinson. You attended one of our events last month at the Plaza. You'll recall the earlier part of the evening, I'm sure. We've had a chance to vet you and would like to invite you to use our service.

"There's complete catering for up to twenty persons. Any desired foods, beverages, tabs, smokes or injectables, as well as compliant participants. No limits, and no repercussions. We provide all consumables, staff, and rooms, and remedies for hangovers and overdoses, which are skilfully administered."

We were sitting at a cocktail table in a starkly modern hotel bar, all blacks and whites and angular furniture. Half-drunken voices lapped at us like angry surf. I leaned backward. "I remember that party, Miss Manners…"

"Call me Missy, please."

"Missy. Not saying I did join in, but why would I want another orgy?"

"Orgy has such messy connotations. We create sensory overload of your most excessive desires for up to forty-eight hours. Our staff monitors your vitals throughout to ensure maximum sensory input and purging and counteractions as necessary to keep your system humming. With friends of your choice or alone."

"And you thought I'd be interested again?"

"You were a vigorous participant with more than one of our entertainments."

"I thought the party was anonymous. Who said you could check up on me?"

Missy reached over and stroked my hand. "Don't be upset. Because of the discreet nature of our service we operate only by referral. We asked the host of that event if he thought you would be a good candidate for membership. His comment, as I recall, was 'no one badder.'"

My turn to smile. I was either being played or was the butt of a bad joke. "And Harry died a month afterwards."

"Of cancer. It was his farewell bash."

I sipped my martini. "So if I were to ask for three women of varying races, each missing one breast, heroin suitable for snorting, wormwood absinthe and mamushi sake, a bed suspended on bungee cords, and a spray hose olive oil dispenser, no problem?"

Missy's smile just perceptibly hardened. "Left or right breasts?"

"Right."

"It would take us about two weeks to find and recruit the women, unless you were happy with either side of the chest flat, in which case ten days."

I kept smiling. She was really good at playing a sucker. "And what would all of that cost?"

"Assuming a suite at a five-star hotel, a two-day run, and a staff of no more than ten, the initial estimate would be $130,000, subject to slight adjustment."

Missy stared at me briefly, then reached into her clutch purse and took out a cell phone. She activated it and turned on a video. "The sound is off, and faces and body art are blacked out. It's a highlights reel of your previous event. You have the starring role."

I watched jump cuts of myself gorging on greasy food and rich desserts, snorting coke, sex together with two women (I looked pathetically pudgy and clumsy), then staffer-induced regurgitation, pill taking, more eating, a lot more, strawberries, oysters, every food thought to be aphrodisiac; the two women again, different postures and orifices; heroin and mamushi sake... I snapped it off.

I sputtered. "That's blackmail!"

"No, it's only your demo tape. We couldn't survive without guaranteeing confidentiality. Keep the phone if you like. We'll be erasing your master file as soon as we're finished here."

"What if I just wanted to watch other gluttonous people getting it on?"

"Afraid not. We handle participants, not voyeurs. I suspect your experience would satisfy several major items on your bucket list while you're still young enough to enjoy them."

"I was kidding about the missing breasts."

"I wasn't," she said. "Almost any request that doesn't injure others or yourself is in play. We handled one event recently that included a sedated female tiger."

Possibilities began to percolate through me. "That's a lot of money."

"It's a designer experience that pegs every one of your red lines without harm. If you wanted to reminisce we can provide Hollywood quality action video, edited to show you in the most flattering ways. You've already had your test drive, you know how overwhelming it is."

She sat back. "There's no need to decide now, you'll want time to think up your optimum experience and decide on guests. Just call me on that number when you're ready. It's the only way to reach me." She laid down cash for the tab and picked up her clutch. "Please finish your drink, Mr. Robinson. On me." Missy stood up and turned away without shaking hands.

I stared at my gin martini. My love of excess screamed 'yes,' but I was dubious. Too dubious. I picked her card up off the table. Miss Manners. What a hustle. I dropped her card into the gin, stood up and walked toward the exit. Before I reached the door, I knew I was making a mistake, ran back to the table and pulled the card out. Ink stained my fingers. The phone number had run and smudged, making it unreadable.

I cursed sub-vocally and sat back down. The waiter came over but I waved him off. I pulled out my phone and typed Miss Manners into the search feature. All I found was crap about good manners. I plugged in Excess Catering and saw nothing significant.

It's been two months, and even with a plunge into the dark web I've come up blank. I find myself watching the video of my fumbling first attempts, saddened by how much more excessive it could have been.

Pigswill

Tracy Lee-Newman

Go on, love; you deserve it. Just one piece of chocolate. One small bar of chocolate. Because of the gas bill. To make you feel good.

And crisps. One bag of crisps for the crap day at work. For Lucy and pals in the staff room, their whispers and snickers. One bar of chocolate and one bag of crisps.

And maybe the ice cream. That smidgen of ice cream. Best finish the tub so the diet can re-start tomorrow.

And cheese. Just a sliver. The one with the holes in; more air then than fat. Cheese for the gas bill, the crap day at work and the bloke at the bank who ignored your best smile.

And a biscuit to go with the cheese. A biscuit or seven.

And bread.

Bread and butter; lots of butter; salted, melted, dripping butter. Peanut butter. Jam. And here you are eating the jam from the jar, so you may as well go the whole hog now, Miss Lardface. You may as well order the takeout – the ribs and the pizza and cookies, and all for the gas bill, the crap day at work and that bloke at the bank who couldn't just smile at you, bastard. But then, take a look at yourself. Think: Well, why would he?

Feel good, hon?

Feel better?

So say it.
Say: never again. Never ever again.
Think: next time it will be for something worthwhile.

The Means

Cynthia Leslie-Bole

He stares at her as though unmoved, and says nothing. A jagged silence hangs densely between them. She rotates the ring around and around on her finger, mirroring the spinning of her mind.

She waits for a response. He gives her none, making her squirm hot-faced in response to his iciness. She bites back the need to explain, rationalize, justify, painfully aware of his criticism that she can never say anything that is direct or clear, that she always has to fill the air with tangles of words, then add more words to qualify those tangles.

She practiced repeatedly yesterday, pacing around the kitchen table until she got her message honed down to its essence, and she delivered it as planned, feeling proud of its brevity: "I want a divorce." And now she waits for a full, agonizing minute before finally caving in and demanding, "Well? Say something, dammit!"

He lifts his pinot and takes a deliberate sip as though assessing the vintage and bouquet of the wine. He carefully sets down the glass on the white tablecloth then he says in a flat voice, "Do you plan to tell me why?" Again he looks at her impassively, like he is only mildly interested in the response.

She says, "You know why. I have told you a million times what I want and need, and you have not been willing to listen, or change, or create a relationship that works for both of us.

We don't need to go over it all again. I'm done, Brian. Done trying. Done explaining. Done hoping. Done with the one-way street."

He takes a precisely-sized bite of arugula salad, and she can hear the spiced walnuts being crushed by his molars. She hates his trained and restrained appetites, would just once like to see him let loose with honest gluttony.

He swallows, dabs his mouth with his napkin, and says, "You know you can't just declare that, right? You know that you have no money of your own, that my salary is all you've got, that you wouldn't have a place to live. Hell, you probably wouldn't even get the kids since you started up with that woman while we're still married. And I need to agree and sign papers for it to go through. What would make me want to do that, Karen? It would be a crime against humanity to unleash you on the world, and you might even be a danger to yourself. Your name probably appears in the dictionary under the definition of loose cannon... I won't do it, Karen, and I'm pleased to say you can't make me."

She stops twisting her napkin under the table and lays her hands down on either side of her untouched plate, pressing down firmly to hide the tremor. She catches the eye of the waiter and nods for the check then looks back at this man. Instead of responding to his taunts, or giving in to his bullying as she has for nineteen years, or crying and yelling and making herself look deranged as she occasionally has out of desperation, she pauses, inhales and exhales, then replies by taking a business card out of her purse and laying it carefully beside his plate. She notices him noticing the new polish on her fingernails and withdraws her hand.

She sits up straighter, then says, "Brian, you have failed to realize that I am not asking you for a divorce. I am telling you that I am getting a divorce. My attorney Ingrid Lake will be contacting you. I advise you not to mess with her. She is a great white shark, and she will eat you alive if necessary."

For the first time, his blasé demeanor cracks. His face flushes and his eyes flash, but then he shrugs and smiles because he knows that rankles her more than anything. "I sincerely doubt it," he says, still holding her gaze while reaching for the check.

But she pulls the tab firmly from his grasp, lays a crisp $500 bill on top, and stands up. "Keep the change. Don't underestimate me, Brian," she says. "I have the means."

His teeth grind as he watches her walk away. His fingers trace the bill with a new question in their movement, and the remainder of his meal lies forgotten.

Edward takes his picnic on the bus

Sarah Salway

I keep my bag on the next seat so I can dip into it every now and then, pull out a silver foil-wrapped package and …
… ohhh …
… a hard boiled egg with …
… yes …
… a twist of salt.

To tell the truth, I've often thought about leaving the egg behind after those two women complained about the smell that one time.

"I thought he was farting, Caroline."

"I didn't like to think."

They were giggling as if I was an entertainment.

"Oh my god, Caroline," the loud one said. "He's got a chicken leg now."

He-he-he-he-he.

And so I didn't gnaw down to the bone as I normally did.

"Caroline, it's a, what is it, can you see?"

I neatly folded the silver paper.

"It's a fucking pineapple, Caroline."

After the egg comes smoked salmon sandwiches, the thinnest brown bread, a scraping of butter followed by a shake of black pepper. I delve into my bag and squeeze slightly although I'm sure I've got the lemon.

These are things someone like Caroline wouldn't know. How much these touches matter. Such as the little sprig of dill with the salmon today. Just enough to tickle my mouth and surprise me.

No, don't think of Caroline today. Breathe deeply. Then into the bag and.

Cream.

Pastry.

A layer of raspberry jam.

Sugar.

Sugar me, mille-feuille.

Ahhh.

This isn't a picnic for the faint-hearted. This is a feast. Hours every night just to make sure it's perfect. And in the morning, I close my eyes to surprise myself, as from a possible choice of twenty, I limit myself to only ten foil-wrapped packages to take. Not eleven. Not nine.

It's taken years to be this self-disciplined.

Now the cake is finished, I pull out the pineapple.

I don't eat it. Who do you think I am? No, it provides the element of drama needed at a certain point in every meal. In Georgian times, they'd hire pineapples out for parties as a centrepiece for the table.

But today I have a different drama in mind.

Because it's now I search for that mystery package I found in the fridge this morning. I place the pineapple on top of my bag so it almost reaches my shoulder. I can feel its foliage stroke my shoulder as I opened the packa…

ALIVE!

Crawling. White. Bloodless.

The lamb chop I had lightly grilled with rosemary months ago.

A grain of rice climbs across to the pineapple before I recover myself. Scrunch the whole package in my hands so I can capture the maggots, the meat, the foil before throwing it behind me.

I lurch forward, stumble down the stairs. Someone presses the bell, but the shouting and screaming forces the bus to a halt anyway.

It's then I start to walk home.

There's an orange waiting patiently for me in my bag and I need to clean my mouth out.

Just Silly Things I Do with Food

Noah Grabeel

Silly thing I do with food #3: I eat leftover pizza cold.

Silly thing I do with food #4: I eat leftover fried chicken cold. Because it's faster than heating it up.

Silly thing I do with food #6: I'm an expert at buffets. You just can't beat all-you-can-eat for $8.74 a head, including tax. As a kid, my family needed the help. A website once told me, at the age of eleven, about how to make the most of a buffet. You go for the protein first, then veggies, and finally you go for the carbs and sugar if you want it. Your stomach doesn't fill as fast if you end with carbs. If you keep up the pace, you can even make sure you get more than enough so that by bedtime you're over the bloating but not hungry until the subsidized breakfast program at school.

Silly thing I do with food #10: If I run out of milk while cooking or baking, I use whatever coffee creamer I have on hand. Sure, peppermint mocha potatoes gratin sounds disgusting, which it is, but what am I supposed to do? Waste perfectly good potatoes and cheese? Do you know how much they cost?

Silly thing I do with food #11: I throw wrappers in the back of the trash can so that my housemates don't see them pile up if I'm being a little bit bad one night and finish an entire box in one sitting.

Silly thing I do with food #20: I plan out my plate. Spinach and peas, all the gross stuff, go first. I save the delicious stuff for last so I can end on a yummy note. The only exception is for fries. There must always be a remainder of fries at the end of a meal. This is just a failsafe, on the off-chance I cannot clean my plate. I would not want to waste more nutritional food on my plate because I filled up on fries. I try to be healthy.

Silly thing I do with food #38: I clean my plate. It's a calculation of energy provided, energy consumed, and energy wasted, and I need perfect 100% completion. Every speck of food is cultivated, harvested, and prepared with so much human effort. Watching bits fall into the disposal feels like a little part of that energy and those people who prepared it are gone too.

Silly thing I do with food #75: Food carries emotion. It's like medicine. Happy foods are mac and cheese, bagels with schmear, and chocolate covered almonds. Sobering foods are things like acai bowls and kale chips or dried apricots. I haven't figured out what lentils are yet.

Silly thing I do with food #86: Food is a crime and a reward all in one. The calories are damning, but the taste is a gift. Except I use it as a reward for other things like sending out unrequited job applications or a shitty night at the club. Except, there's still the crime of calories, so I have to figure out what to eat to even it all out. Except, then it gets more complicated going on from there.

Silly thing I do with food #92: In an effort to get control over my eating habits, I create elaborate traps with other items in the pantry. I don't bury junk food or make it inaccessible. If I did that, the hassle would be too much, and I'd leave them in plain sight once I found them. I can't be trusted with that kind of unrestricted access. Instead I leave the box of snack cakes open next to a cereal box that is on its side (the shelf is too short). Moving the box to a diagonal position creates more space for my hand to retrieve a treat. One quick slide of the box lets me have easy access, but otherwise the junk food is hidden from view. I eat fewer treats because it still takes enough effort for me to pause and reflect on my life choices. Is it really worth it? Why do I need this snack cake? I'm deterred by the extra effort, which, honestly, feels almost magical when you're tempted like I am with the annoying necessity of eating on a daily basis. When I open the pantry, I don't see a smiling, cherubic face on the box or thick spongy snack cakes with a smooth layer of icing. Instead I see the cans of tuna that are part of my new diet, and canned tuna in water is about the unsexiest food I can think of.

Local BBQ

Jemshed Khan

Waft of smoke and sizzle greets. Cashier half-yells, *May I take your order*. Behind her the kitchen boasts red-tiled splendor – fattened calves whittled down to a glaze of ribs. She loads my fiberglass tray with a short end heavy sauce, yammer pie, paper boats of fat cut fries, sliced beef stacked between white bread, platter of onion rings and a brew.

Soon I tear a rib from its brethren. Lift it dripping to my face; nostrils sniff, flare. Saliva gluts my mouth. Licked lips part, incisors whet. Feast on tender pork seared in sauce. Fingers, teeth, tongue, strip every bit to bone.

Then, this burning in my chest – not just hot sauce trying to digest. Feels like my last heart attack: cold sweat, palpitations. Maybe angina pectoris.

Place sublingual nitrocyglerin. At least the pain's easing and breathing better too. Pulse feels even, good – mouth another succulent, wash it down with beer, slush some fries in tangy BBQ, shove 'em all down the chute.

Folie à Deux

Iris N. Schwartz

Over two hundred seventy dollars' worth of groceries. For one September weekend. One couple. Thirteen plastic bags' worth. Shoved into Toyota trunk. Spillover in back seat? Bulging-bag, frozen-chocolate babies, secured with belts. Fried, buttery, and/or cheesy children? Safe in said trunk.

Calvert and LorrieAnn rushed their sedentary selves onto worn front seats. As if synchronized, both turned to face the back. Both leaned over, maniacally searched for victual treasure.

Must have taken twenty seconds — tops — to locate diet goodies, but for Cal and Lorrie they might have gone spelunking through an endless pitch-black cave.

"Cal," Lorrie spoke without looking up, "where are they? Do you think we left them behind?"

Cal shook one plastic bag, tamped down his smile. "Relax, Li'l Lore. I have a few boxes here."

Lorrie despised Cal's "Li'l" nickname for her, especially as the term hadn't even fit (ha, ha) fourteen months ago, when they'd first met — when she'd been sixty pounds lighter.

The currently two-hundred-and-five-pound, dark blonde did not want to remember how *nearly slim* she'd been the day they'd met. Nor did Lorrie want rage coloring her face as she recalled the roughly five-hundred-pound Cal selfie he unashamedly thrust between her face and her half-pound cheeseburger during their first meal together. He'd also described gruesomely detailed steps of the gastric bypass he'd undergone about two years before they'd met.

At the time — at their first dinner out — she'd graciously listened, thought: *how brave of him to share this private trauma.*

Lorrie now realized that Cal as much as told her his former self was still a large-looming possibility. He had warned her, but she'd been speaking the language of romance ever since that afternoon fourteen months ago, had willed herself not to be bilingual until, perhaps, today.

No, Lorrie again chose not to think. She needed fudgsicles to numb tongue, throat, brain. Needed an avalanche to bury…Cal? Herself? Both?

During this getaway weekend Cal didn't need to fear being alone with his fiancée. The Spartan quality of his parents' upstate New York bungalow would likely keep Lorrie uncomfortable both days.

Though very early September it was icy-cold upstate, indoors and out. The bungalow's water was still turned off. Furniture was sparse, amenities non-existent: a small piece that doubled as dining and writing table; two hard-backed, uncushioned chairs; one twin bed in each of the two bedrooms. No rugs. No television. No books. Yellowing magazines going back two decades or three. Two blankets, two pillows.

Unlikely even Lorrie would demand sex in this environment.

The next day, if all went as he'd planned for the night before — night into dawn shoveling down store-bought fried chicken; mac and cheese; and family-sized tubs of French vanilla pudding — Cal and Lorrie would awaken in separate, cold-as-Cal's-heart bedrooms, with carbohydrate hangovers they hadn't experienced since the first time they'd slept and eaten together.

Lorrie had wanted a weekend trip for the two of them, alone. That's what Cal would give her — emphasis on 'alone'. His laughter chilled his bones, rattled his cavernous heart.

It woke Lorrie from choco-fudge quiescence. She wiped her mouth and chin: brown stickiness adhered to her pudgy palms. Looked at her pants, straining at the thighs: still-cool fudgsicle droplets dotted dark denim. And at her feet, on Toyota floor? Piles of wrappers frantically ripped, intermingled with gnawed sticks. Many sticks: more than could fit in one, two, or three frozen dessert containers.

At her left, slumped over five empty fudgsicle boxes, Cal in his dark brown "puffy" jacket. Dark brown, he'd advised her, showed few stains. Puffy "accentuated" his "football-player physique."

"O.K., time to get these groceries to the bungalow." Lorrie tapped his forearm. "Come on, you'll sleep it off inside." No response. She started to pick up dessert detritus from the floor. Stopped when Cal nearly fell on top of her.

It was bitter outside, and the Toyota's windows were closed, but families in the parking lot clearly heard Lorrie's penetrating screams.

Flying

Townsend Walker

Not that I want to, but I'm getting on the cross-town 22 Fillmore bus. She called, said I had to come.

"It's over between us," I told her. "Why drag it out?"

I hate going to her place; it's a sty. But she kept on and on. Finally I agreed, seemed the quickest way to end her nattering.

On the bus, I sit down next to blonde pixie hair, green eyes, red tank top, torn jeans. Not bad actually. Head's bopping to whatever's coming through her ear buds.

I bump her a bit sitting down. Get this look from her: *You're in my space, dude.* I ignore it. Stare straight ahead.

Then she pokes me in the shoulder. I turn; she's mouthing, *You're crowding me, porker.*

I'm not که big, not a glutton, a bit over average maybe: 3 feet, 355. No reason to poke and swear. I slide over. Pretty much in the aisle now. Not comfortable, beads of sweat running down my nose.

The bus stops: a lady with bags in both hands comes up the aisle, bangs me in the back, I topple into cute tank top.

Before I could say excuse me, she rips the buds from her ears and screams, "You pig!"

"I am not a pig!"

The scrawny haggish woman one seat back, "Yes you are."

I slump, then slowly, slowly get off the bus, wishing, wishing I could fly.

Chain of Events

Mark Budman

1. *Going Bananas*

Henry counts the number of different cereal types on the supermarket shelf. Twenty-three. But if you remove everything with sugar or salt, there will be only one left. That's life. Seemingly a great variety but if you want to be different, you have severely limited choices. As a thirty-third generation magician and a certified contrarian of the second highest degree, Henry knows.

A fat girl, who follows her mother's cart, picks up a ripe banana from the shelf. The girl bites off a little piece and throws the rest on the floor. Henry can't let it go.

"Look what your daughter has done," he says sternly. He's a Good Samaritan. But though he's right, he still expects the mother to yell at him or maybe even call the police. A week ago, when he told an obese woman she shouldn't eat bacon, she called the store manager. People who practice gluttony are touchy.

Instead of yelling, the mother picks up the remainder of the banana and puts it back on the shelf. "I'm sorry," she says.

Henry melts. This woman is different. Being different is so sweet.

He picks up the banana. Most of it is still covered by the skin. It smells delicious. He breaks off and discards the piece where the girl bit off, and eats the rest. It has practically no salt. Henry, the third generation teacher, knows. He deposits the peel back on the shelf and heads for the cash register.

He queues behind an old man with a box of full-strength Coke in his cart. 150 calories per can. Henry will scold him now. They both made their choices, but only one of them is the right one. And Henry always wins in the end, even if he has to return to the empty house, and even if his much-berated cat escaped through the window eons ago. But not before she opened the parakeet's cage and let the bird go.

2. *Beholding the Stars*

The man from the supermarket—his name is Rudolph—returns home with the box of Coke. He just had a fight with a weird guy in the grocery store. It was a draw.

Rudolf drinks almost the entire can of Coke, empties the rest into the sink, and watches the bubbles rise. Rudolph lost a pound in a month and is proud of himself.

Later that night, Rudolph stands on a narrow ledge in a hall about four stories tall but without the roof. Stars shine above his head. A black funereal curtain runs along the wall behind him. Below him, a woman and a robot are having a fist fight on top of a horse with the fur of a poodle. A woman is even skinnier than Rudolph, which is hard. The robot, with a bunch of clicking relays inside its clear head, looks like it came from a nineteen-fifties movie Rudolph loved to watch as a kid. Its limbs are hydraulic.

Rudolph sympathizes with the woman because she is flesh and blood, almost like him, and the robot is mostly steel.

The robot seems brand-new and well-oiled. Retro, Rudolf thinks. Retro comes from French rétro, abbreviation of retrograde, which means "retrograde". Retro is in fashion in some circles. The woman is more agile, though.

Rudolph records the proceedings on his phone. He thinks about all the possible allegories and metaphors. He knows that the "allegory" is spelled with two Ls, but wonders if the "metaphor" is spelled with an E at the end. It would be if it were French. They love soft endings.

When the fight is over, a bunch of uniformed men enter the hall and are trying to catch the fighters with nets. Eventually, they all run out.

Rudolph can't maintain his balance for much longer. After all, he's 66. An age where sex and acrobatics are still desirable but the stamina is waning.

He explores his choices.

Choice one: to climb up the curtain and through the window to the roof and then to the stars that he could see through the windows.

Choice two: try to tear the curtain and gently lower himself to the floor.

He goes with choice two, tears the curtain with his teeth and drops down. The curtain detaches from the wall and Rudolph finds himself in a free fall. He whistles a brave tune but in fact, he is not feeling brave. Flipping over in the air, he turns to the stars for the last time but, curiously, they are growing instead of staying the same size. In fact, they're growing so fast and so large they swallow him whole in a big explosion.

The Big Lunch

Elaine Barnard

I bundle Father into his heavy parka and hat, woolen socks and warm boots. It is winter in Southern California, but my father always feels he is back in China where winters can be fierce, the snow as high as his boots and his head, even with earmuffs, still cold. "Father," I urge, "come have your breakfast. It will be hours before lunch. We do not know what the Marriott will serve, if it will be enough for you."

My father still has a huge appetite even though he is nearing his ninetieth year. I have prepared his favorite spicy fried rice with chicken. I pour his tea. "Oolong?" he sniffs as if he were at home in his garden smelling the morning flowers. My father was a devoted gardener, out every morning trimming and planting. Now we live in a small apartment in Garden Grove, a misnomer because there are no groves and hardly any gardens. But we are near the Chinese Senior Center where my father plays Mahjong with other men whose wives are dead and their children departed.

While Father slurps his tea, I dress in jeans and sweaters. Lately I have begun to feel cold as well. I think it must be the arthritis that has plagued me since I retired from my import business. Now I have more time to visit doctors who tell me it was my work that caused my pain. I guess I never stopped working. Even in my sleep I dreamt of tea, green and black, aromatic and bitter that I imported from China and sold to shops throughout Orange County and Los Angeles, driving miles on the freeway every day to fill the orders. "Why don't you hire a delivery boy?" my father often muttered. "No, I must see my customers in person, chat with them, drink tea, eat roasted chestnuts and almond cookies. That way they are more than numbers in my ledger."

Some criticized me because I worked so hard, made so much money. But in China we did not have the luxury of not working hard. So many people, everyone scrambling their way up, desperate to not be left behind.

Today we are attending an appreciation lunch, presented by an annuity company in which I invested many thousands of dollars to ensure my later years. I will have an income until I die. But to tell the truth, sometimes my body hurts so much with the arthritis I want to die and leave my money to Father, who would undoubtedly gamble it away at Mahjong.

After I help him into the bathroom and make certain he is clean, I pack my purse with plastic containers. No food will go to waste. What I cannot eat I will save for Father who never seems to have enough.

Finally we are ready. I help him into the car. He is healthy but he is slow and bent with age. I buckle his safety belt as if he were a child; pat his cheek to make him smile, and then climb in behind the wheel. I boost myself on a cushion so I can see the road ahead. Being only four feet, five inches makes driving any car difficult. My feet don't touch the pedals. The mechanics fixed the pedals so my shoes could reach them. Father tells me I am no bigger than a doll; "Shushi, you still have time to grow," he used to say. But that time has long passed.

We exit from the freeway. The morning sun blinds me. Even with my glasses I can't make out the numbers on the buildings. We pass the Hyatt and the Wyndham, the Residence Inn and the Motel 8 but nowhere is the Marriott.

"Are you sure you have the right address?" Father mumbles as he munches the fortune cookies I've brought for his snack. "I do not like these fortunes." He tosses the papers out the car window.

"It is the address they gave me on the phone." I feel a headache coming on. As my Tai Chi master instructed, I press my free hand to my temples to relieve the pressure.

"Maybe you did not hear right." He wipes crumbs from his mouth.

"My hearing is fine." I gulp some water from the thermos at my side.

"But maybe you only think it is fine." He rattles the bag, hoping to find another cookie. "You should take a test."

"I've taken a test." My palms feel sweaty on the steering wheel.

"That was last year." He licks the bag.

"Father, please, I have to concentrate."

"You should have dropped me at the Senior Center. I miss my friends."

"You said you wanted to have the big lunch." Sweat stains my underarms. We are both overdressed for noon in Southern California where the temperature rises in mid-day, making the car an inferno. I never turn on the air-conditioning as that would displease him. He might get chilled.

"Do you have any more fortunes?" He crushes the empty bag.

"No, you don't want to spoil your lunch."

"What lunch? We'll never have any lunch the way you're driving."

"We will. We just have to keep looking. The Marriott has to be somewhere."

"I'm hungry," he grumbles, patting his paunch. "I want to go back to China."

"I want to go back to China too." My head begins to throb. The air is thick with smog. The car behind me beeps with irritation. I give him the finger. He's on my tail now, blaring his horn. Then he's beside me, glaring through his window. I pay no attention and try to speed up. He cuts me off.

"Look," Father blurts, "MANDARIN KING-LUNCH SPECIALS."

The restaurant is on the wrong side of the street so I make an illegal U-turn and pull into the empty lot.

"We will have the big lunch." My father hurries to unbuckle the seat belt straining across his belly.

I am no longer hungry. My stomach is a hollow well of exhaustion. I drag his walker from the trunk of the car and place it beside the passenger door. Extending my arms, I try to pull him from the car and steady him beside the walker. Clinging to the walker, he totters toward the gleaming letters, the lotus blossoms and carp swimming in the pond as if he were the Mandarin King and I his faithful servant. He does not notice the "Closed" sign on the door.

Food for Thought

Larry Lefkowitz

Except for her ironclad rules: if it smelled bad, she would not eat it; if it was improperly cooked, she would not eat it; if it was out of season, she would not eat it – Victoria's taste in food did not suffer from limitation. French, Hungarian, Greek, what-have-you fare she enjoyed like an international gourmet food aficionado; yet she kept a soft spot in her heart's stomach for traditional Jewish meals: noodle soup, brisket with tzimmes, chopped herring and onions and chicken fat, chopped liver, cholent, kugel, borscht, kreplach are just some of the cuisine I remember her ingesting at one time or another.

Victoria was a voracious meat eater. At times she seemed bent on sucking out the very marrow of life. Once, I mocked her proclivity for eating well by quoting Max Beerbohm, "The lower one's vitality, the more sensitive one is to great art." "Extremely droll," she dismissed this, adding, "I will only refrain from eating famously when it becomes the greatest of my remaining sins." This left me speechless – and wondering about the remaining sins. Yet her remark seemed too polished for Victoria – I suspected she had stolen it from whom? – Cleopatra in some American movie or TV version of 'Caesar and Cleopatra'? This led to the thought that in her afterlife, Victoria, like an ancient Egyptian queen, would be grateful for the food left in the sepulcher for the deceased's long journey through eternity. On another occasion, I chided her on her vigorous appetite, so opposite to my cuisine maigre (she, like Bloom, enjoyed eating; I, like Molly, dispatched my food without ceremony). Irritated, she called me a *bitere tsibele* (literally 'a bitter onion' but meaning 'a wet blanket'), and then went on to lump me as a "culinary proletarian", the opposite, I suppose, of a culinary connoisseur. Her attitude to food can be summed up best by the Yiddish morsel *Ven ikh ess, hob ikh zey ale drerd* (When I eat, they can all go to hell).

George Steiner: "Living and eating are indeed absolute necessities, but also bleak and secondary in the light of the exploration and communication of great and final things." For Victoria, the shoe was on the other foot. She even favored culinary imagery. One of her favorites: "You can turn chicken soup into borscht, but you can't turn borscht into chicken soup."

Even if Victoria sulked, it in no way diminished her gusto for eating. Once I chastised her because of her eating habits. Without batting an eye, she replied, "You're a voracious reader – you devour pages faster and more obsessively than I do food." More than once she would urge me, "Eat, Kunzman – if you don't eat, you'll be an empty sack that will fall" or "Don't eat like a bird, Kunzman."

Victoria needed someone to talk to while she ate. Not for mutual conversation (at least not with me). She did most of the talking and most of the eating. But not alone. Never alone. "If I eat alone, the food doesn't taste as good," she explained.

Before leaving the subject of food – which subject I will associate to the end of my days with Victoria, who talked about food in the rare moments when she happened not to be eating any – there should not be overlooked the nexus between food and intimate physical relationship (today called sex); relevant here is an incident involving Victoria. At a fancy reception in honor of some visiting Russian harp player (who was a dead ringer for Gorbachev's wife), Victoria swept down, her aubergine dress bellowing behind her suggesting an eggplant in motion, on a table of *forshpayzn* – hors-d'oeuvres being a comparatively effete synonym on a Yiddish-speaker's tongue – ignored a plate of pickled turnips on crackers and spread a lavish amount of caviar on a cracker, and began to devour it. To me, her escort (I had to rent a tuxedo for the occasion!) Victoria vouchsafed the fact that "the aphrodisiac I prefer is caviar." Despite my distaste for caviar (I'm a herring aficionado), I picked up on the theme and informed her that the 15th-century Arabic poet Nafzavi recommended for use by young men an aphrodisiac recipe consisting of a glass of honey, 20 almonds and 100 pine-nuts; for older men a cocktail of female camel's milk and honey. I added that Scott Fitzgerald was a believer in the use of mandrake for said purposes. Victoria shook her head in impatience, "I'm not surprised that you would bring up a literary aspect even to the subject of aphrodisiacs." Unable to think of a suitable riposte to this, I simply shrugged. But Victoria wasn't finished. "The female camel's milk and honey is for you." I wondered if the husband or partner of the harpist who looked like Gorbachev's wife was on the receiving end of such taunts. Was tartness of tongue endemic to women harpists, like Victoria? Were there men harp players? I couldn't recall one (other than Harpo Marx). Why? I was about to raise the matter with Victoria, but she had, once again, swept down upon the gedekte tishen ("covered tables") laden with food and drink. An action which produced in my mind three thoughts, which followed one another in rapid succession: the first, that when Socrates wanted to condemn a young man for excessive indulgence in luxuries, he called him an opson-eater – someone who ate fancy side-dishes, not bread; his judgment presumably would also encompass young women, or even not-so-young women. In Victoria's defense, however, she favored both the fancy food and the bread. The second thought, less charitable than the first, was that Victoria should be reincarnated as a cow, a creature blessed with four stomachs – what couldn't be digested in the first could be passed on to the second, and so forth. My third thought was of Gombrowicz's observation that the mental exertion of a waiter, who has to remember orders from five tables and not make a mistake, at the same time hurrying about with plates, bottles, sauces, and salads, seemed to him infinitely greater than the exertions of an author trying to arrange the different subtle threads of his plots. (This should put into perspective any reader's complaining: "What is all this going on about food, which has little connection to literature?" Victoria would answer such complaint by emulating a character in Shabtai's 'Past continuance' who, picking up a menu, exclaims, "This is the best literature I know.") During the time I was engaging in these thoughts, Victoria had speared with one hand a delicacy placed in a salver for this purpose and with the other hand had deftly seized a glass of red wine from the tray of a passing waiter and was now noshing vociferously on some pink and blue and green sweetmeat. I decided that it was best not to interrupt her in her favorite pastime.

Eater in the Woods

John Kujawski

I needed a place to dump the dead body and I had my concerns. I had driven to a wooded area near a park where I grew up and I figured it was a good place to serve my needs. After all, not many people hung out there. For one thing, it was a rainy day and people would probably be home where it was warm. The other reason folk stayed away was due to the rumors of a strange animal roaming around.

I had never seen this creature before, whatever it was. Being in the state of Missouri, sometimes people grew bored with their lives and made up weird stories. A big part of me believed them but I still decided to go to that place and take my chances. Since I had a corpse in the trunk, I wanted to get rid of it as quickly as possible.

I decided not to rush things when I walked through the area, though. If someone was wandering around and saw me, I wanted to appear like I was out for a casual stroll. So, I stopped the car on a gravel road and that was exactly what I did. I went into those woods as if I wasn't a threat to anyone. The only thing I brought was my gun. I wasn't a big guy but that gun was the perfect protection. It was the same one I used to kill a man.

I felt very much alive in that wooded location. I didn't see anyone around and all was quiet. The rain was coming down but it was light and it didn't bother me. All I saw were trees and rocks at first. I was about to head to the car to get the body when I realized I had company.

I'm not exactly sure what happened. One minute I was alone and the next moment a giant animal was standing in front of me. It looked like a deer at first but that was just from the size of it. It was brown and it had a large tail and the teeth on the thing were like that of a dinosaur. I knew it wasn't a deer. I was glad I had my gun on me because clearly the rumors about the odd animal were true. I wasn't sure if it was evil or not.

I watched it for a while but then all it seemed to want to do is eat. First it went after a branch of a tree. The beast ate the leaves right off it and then the actual wood as well. It made me think of a dinosaur and the slurping noises it made were ones I would never forget. Next, it started eating leaves off the ground. They were wet leaves but this monster didn't seem to care.

I wondered for a moment if it was a vegetarian but then I noticed a dead squirrel on the ground. Before I knew it that squirrel was gone. I think that freak of nature even swallowed it whole. It didn't seem to be coming towards me at all but it just kept eating. I started to head back to the car and I could hear those slurping noises loud and clear. That was when I came up with an idea.

I wondered if the animal was evil. What it was doing was not a simple matter of having a meal. This was a demonstration of gluttony and I knew that was a sin. I certainly had committed a sin when I took someone's life. The best thing I could think to do was to give it something else to devour.

I opened the trunk of the car and pulled the dead guy out of it. I had him all wrapped up in plastic and he was heavy so I dragged him back into the wooded area. It was what I had planned to do anyway even if I hadn't run into this creepy species. It took most of my strength to pull that body into the woods but eventually I made it back to where I could see that thing again. It was still eating leaves but I had a much better treat for it. I left the body on the ground and took a step back. I thought I was in for quite a show.

My new friend walked right up to the body and I could hear it sniffing through its nose. All of a sudden it let off a horrible sounding squeal, took a look at me, and walked off. It didn't want to eat human flesh. It didn't want anything to do with it at all.

At that point I knew the animal was not a danger to humans. I didn't know what it was but I knew it was nothing bad. I was the only sinner in the woods that day and I was the one who had killed a man.

Candy

Jake Greenblot

Look, I mix some kale and quinoa in with the burritos and barbecue—I do yoga. Well, a couple times. My alarm is useless. I wake up on my own, muttering through mornings, juicing what seems unjuiceable—nigh inedible—and swallow everything down with ascetic aplomb. Then it's off to beat rush hour.

No matter how tight things get (which can range from "Uncomfortably" to "Perilously" to "Siri—Show Me Driving Directions to the Nearest Plasma Donation Center"), the rent is always delivered in full and on time. I'm pretty sure the toner on my W-2 was still warm when I filed our taxes last week.

The windfall—slight-breeze-fall, more accurately—of a couple hundred dollars in refund freshly deposited in the barely-black balance of the bank account, I had drooped through the Save-So-Much with my elbows resting on a creaky cart filled with flax seed, acai, and matcha. Cashew milk. Cauliflower rice. Some organic, non-GMO, gluten-free, low-carb approximation of tortillas—more of a chewy coconut-oil/sawdust/God-knows-what-else homage to the *idea* of a tortilla, really. There had been the scent of taquito samples wafting through the aisles, where vestiges of Christmas were slowly ceding real estate to pre-Valentine's Day chocolates. New Wave bleating through tiny horn-shaped speakers above—what was the name of this band? Bow Wow Wow, that's right.

"That's right." I shrug. Back home. I'm supine on the sofa, my location and position for what I can only estimate has been a good, long while.

"I just don't—"

"You know. Like that song. I Want—"

"No, I got it. I remember. But…" The living room is a kaleidoscopic mélange: shiny wrappers, artificial dyes, opaque plastic bags crinkling at our feet. "But two hundred *dollars*?"

Two hundred four dollars and ninety cents, actually. A few miles away, some kid at the store is re-shelving my forsaken fat-free Greek yogurt and green tea powder, cursing me with every item pulled from the cart I jettisoned near the frozen vegetables in favor of an empty one. From the couch, my words are muffled by cheap chocolate and chewy nougat.

"Hey—in for a penny, right?" Right?

The League of the Loved

Peter Lingard

Just like they did on earth, celebrities here band together. They, we, yeah I suppose I'm one of them, reckon we're still special. Royal types think they're still royal. Actors still perform and singers still rap, warble or shout out their musical efforts, while us musicians pretend we still have a piano to play or a drum to beat. Hi, I'm John Lennon. Welcome to the Ultimate Afterlife. I guess the fact that you're here means it's pointless to mention the Alternate Afterlife; it's not what you'd call a hot topic. Come on! That was funny.

Each day here is a metaphorical Sunday, so those of us who care about our history of heartaches meet on every fourth day. I haven't yet figured out why every fourth day, but it's not as if I'm pushed for time. As I said, we're celebrities of one kind or another. At these meetings the main topic of conversation is the amount of mourning and grieving the living public indulged on whoever died. We even have a list of ranking, The League of The Loved, we call it. It grades those who have been given the greatest amount of after-death adulation. Princess Di has led the league since her death in August ninety-seven but she is in constant fear that someone will soon garner a greater outpouring of emotion. She sees her spiteful mother-in-law as a big threat, despite the woman's age. Di is reported to have said *Anywhere I see suffering, that is where I want to be, doing what I can –* what isn't reported is her post-life addendum, *to ensure they don't outdo me in public mourning when they die.* She constantly frets that Elvis, who died twenty years before her, will slowly overtake her as those who think he's still alive finally succumb to the traumatic truth. There was a time when Di worried about Paul McCartney's one-legged ex seeking revenge after having been dumped. She only relaxed when she realised old Paul had passed the mass adoration age.

I'm chuffed to be in second place. My death at Marc's hand in December nineteen-eighty had 'em out in the millions; flowers and candles, prayers and gifts strewn on streets and pavements all over the world. Not long ago, someone bought a lock of my hair for thirty five thousand, US. I've obviously still got it. I wonder if I can appear in one of Yoko's dreams and give her some new music? As I once said on earth, *Everybody loves you when you're six feet in the ground.*

Winston Churchill is ever a loyal royalist but the thistly man is not pleased to be lower on the chart than a rock and roller like me. "My state funeral in sixty-five was massive," he said to me.

"True," I agreed, "but your funeral was an organised effort." Johnny Kennedy had the same. Look at Jesus. He joined in April of thirty-three – that's zero-thirty-three. Mind, I don't reckon he'd've had much trouble qualifying. *He's* not fussed about my standing. Bloody millions must've been sad when he died, but my position in the chart comes from the spontaneous outpouring of love by the people of *my* day. You know, I once said I'd be bigger than Jesus. America's religious bigots got their balls in a right uproar over it, but look how things've turned out.

Old Winston wasn't happy when he learned my second name.

"Don't fret it," I told him. "I tried to dump it when I was alive. Maybe here I can be known simply as John Ono." Who here would take care of mundane stuff like that? Howard Hughes? Imagine! What was it he said? *The human brain is still undergoing rapid adaptive evolution.* I wonder if he still thinks that now his brain's no longer human? Has he found a nail salon here? We're all bound to slide down the chart sooner or later, as new people arrive. Michael Jackson might have made it to the top had there not been all those shitty revelations, but he still made a showing. Robin Williams caused a bit of a stir. Before he arrived here he asked, *Do you think God gets stoned? I think so...look at the platypus.* He's not told me if they gave him a hard time at the gates. I understand the Queen Mother is here somewhere. They say she can be seen now and then painfully bending to lift the skirts of clouds, looking for bottles of gin she thinks are hidden there. Marilyn Monroe once said, *It's all make believe, isn't it?* You can ask her what she thinks now. You can't miss her; she roams the place, all the while pinching herself. James Dean's here. When on earth he said, *If a man can bridge the gap between life and death, if he can live after he's died, then maybe he was a great man. Immortality is the only true success.* You'll see him wandering around the place with a permanent grin etched on his face. It's a funny mixture we have. Look how Princess Di fretted over David Bowie. I actually saw her twitch when she heard he'd gone toes up. Speaking of Ziggy, I haven't seen him yet, nor that country guy, Glenn Frey. Did you lot die before those two? Have you seen them here somewhere? What about George Michael? I assume he's here, somewhere. You know who I mean, right? Ziggy? Glenn Frey of the Eagles? Wham. Would you know them? Perhaps they're still going through the entry exams and acceptance procedures. Prince should be there by now. He really turned the world purple when he checked out. Even if he or Ziggy don't top the league, there's the like of Justin Bieber to watch out for, especially if he snuffs it in some spectacular manner within the next couple of years. You'll soon be wondering what people, those still alive and kicking, would think if they could be a fly on a cloud and overhear our petty jealousies about where we stand in our League of The Loved. Would they stop with the flowers and the rest of the rubbish, or do they think their showings of adoration somehow link them to us? There must be some who assume we're watching their actions and think we thank them. Well, you guys were there not that long ago; did any of you feel the need to show your grief publicly? More calculating humans might believe they're amassing heavenly brownie points. Have you newbies realised yet that their manufactured grief is a lie and could cause points to be deducted from their accounts? It's okay, don't fret it. You lot are already in.

I bump into my mum every now and then, but we move in different circles. Earthly family connections mean nothing here; everyone's their own person. I see George occasionally, but we don't hang together.

Thing is, I can't get rid of this gig, even though I know next to nothing about stuff I wasn't directly involved in on earth. I know a bit about Nelson Mandela and Mother Teresa and other good folks but not enough to tell newbies like you about them. To be honest, most of them aren't interested in The League anyhow. Why would they be when they didn't get the adulation some entertainers and royalty got. That should tell you summat about life as we know it, eh? Like Winston Churchill. I came across him because me mum named me after him. But I didn't learn any more about him than I knew on earth; how he won the war for the good guys and all that stuff. Mind, there's some here hate his guts – not that they can do anything about it. Peace is enforced; there's gangs of angels, a bit like bikies really, who materialise at a first angry word or look. I should write a song.

So, every day I meet the newbies and tell them all this shit and I worry it's what I'll be doing 'til eternity. Eternal gluttony.

Gentlemen in Waiting

Tom Fegan

"Open up. It's the police and we have a warrant for your arrest," shouted the officer. With no response from the upstairs apartment next door to me the next noise I heard was their crashing through. The melee interrupted my morning coffee and I stood frozen, listening to swearing and struggling as bodies slammed into the wall and onto the floor.

I peeked out my front window through the shades and saw my neighbor Terry Cruz handcuffed and dragged from his apartment. Moments later the patrol car left with him in custody.

This shattering event had transgressed due to the overlapping relationships my other next-door neighbor Caroline Suggs had with three young men. Caroline was a blonde with a degree in Secretarial Administration who preferred being a temp office worker than being employed in a steady position. "Something new all the time," she sparkled. Caroline's insatiable desire to satisfy her whims and wants meant she had to keep her men in waiting at bay; but it got her what she wanted.

As a retired and widowed postal inspector who had downsized to apartment living, I watched and listened and only indulged in passing conversation with them: their actions told the story.

Everett Jacks was a well-groomed banking account manager at the neighborhood bank where I was a customer. Jacks' tall height, lean frame and sharp appearance were set off by a wide smile and an outgoing personality. He always greeted me anywhere with, "How are you?"

He spoke to me about his golf game, his serious intentions with Caroline along with their plans for theater, film, dancing, or dinner with his parents at their private club. And he also spoke about David Lewis, an IRS employee he knew who visited her only on Sunday afternoons for a matinee, special event, and dinner or evening church services.

David had kindly visited me once before leaving her one Sunday evening, after she had told him of my past postal career. We compared jobs and swapped stories about federal enforcement. A bespectacled man of average height and quiet thought and demeanor, all he got from Caroline was a frontal hug.

But Terry Cruz ... his jet black Silverado and its freight train horn blasting his machismo, served Caroline's other needs. He boasted of a home business that was really a pyramid scheme, where products are hardly sold and the desired result is to get three people to get three people to get three people. Well, his *real* clientele appeared at different hours of the day and night softly knocking at his door and creeping silently way. I was amused and knew the deal: most apartment complexes have a dope dealer in residence, and Cruz fit the profile.

Everett Jacks would leave with kisses and endearments from Caroline at conclusion of their Saturday night date ... then Cruz's shadow would slither past my front window. A rhythmic knock would follow, then her door would fan open and shut. It was an amusing counterpoint to my weekly viewing of *Saturday Night Live*.

The bust made local news and connected Cruz with an interstate drug cartel. I visited the bank and Jacks waved me into his office. He closed the door behind me and shook his head bitterly.

"I'm through with her," he began, "to think I wanted to marry her. I'm embarrassed and so is my family. She had to know about him." He looked at the floor, collecting his thoughts. "I saw him go into her apartment the last time I was there. I was steamed and haven't called her since. Then this happens." I nodded in agreement and consoled him with the fact that there were others and not to get serious too quick. "Poor David," he added, "I know he is still hanging around her. He's a glutton for punishment."

While I drove back to my apartment, I reviewed the conversation in my head and smiled at what Jacks didn't know. David Lewis was employed by the IRS as a Criminal Investigator. He had met Cruz while visiting Caroline and immediately concluded Cruz's game. After we had met I kept him informed of Cruz's movements, maintaining contact by cell phone. David sadly admitted he was smitten by her, but realized all he could do was keep her out of the investigation and make a convincing argument that she was only sideline sex for Cruz. "I've learned my lesson," David had shared.

Caroline broke her lease and started her move, and was back in business as three different lads helped her relocate. One with a van got the boxes. Another rented a U-Haul and with help of a friend moved her furniture.

The last time I saw her she had put her clothes and other necessaries in her car. She paused, shrugged her shoulders, slid into the vehicle, and just before she started the engine a familiar horn blast rocked the neighborhood. The black Silverado blocked her car; she jumped out and waved excitedly.

Cruz pushed the passenger door open and cried, "Come on!" She rushed towards the truck and climbed in beside him.

As they raced away the horn blasted again. I stood by the window puzzled at the game she played with others and puzzled at her choice in men. I wondered which one of them, Cruz or Caroline, was being taken for a ride.

Her car was towed a week later.

The Recent History of the Sánchez Family Tragedies: Part II

Guilie Castillo Oriard

Maybe first love really is indelible. Maybe eight is too old to become a father's son—and little Anselmo, your grandfather, was well versed at being a mama's boy (whether because of the circumstances he was born to or his own nature—a flaw in his character, a quirk in a strand of DNA). In any case, the marriage was a mistake.

By all accounts, the courtship between Maura and The Doctor was short. Maybe even in those days, when propriety ruled Mexico with a tighter fist than it does today, allowances could be made for unwed mothers. Maybe the widowed Doctor Sánchez was Maura's last chance at respectability (she turned twenty-seven the week before the wedding)—and at escaping the calvary of shame her life had become since the night Papa caught her with the German boy.

The beatings began on the honeymoon, and never stopped. He never laid a hand on his own children, but Maura—and Anselmo, of course—were never safe. Maura tried to negotiate: *hit me, not him*, but that vein of self-sacrifice pushed The Doctor over the edge; he did hit her, as hard as he dared, and then he moved on to Anselmo. *Bastard. Child of sin. Worthless leech.*

Sometimes the boy got away, his heart a tangle of guilt (for letting his mother take the blows meant for him) and hatred (for the man and for himself, for his cowardice) and relief (for having dodged this beating) and anxiety (because the beating wasn't avoided, just postponed). Sometimes, especially as he grew older and more practiced, more impervious (more cynical?), he didn't run. Better now than later. Then it was over and life could go on.

And yet Maura never left The Doctor. Certainly in those days it was much harder to escape an abusive relationship. Hell, most relationships *were* abusive. A good hiding was considered the cornerstone of discipline. And—well, hadn't The Doctor agreed to adopt Anselmo legally, give him his name? A generic Sánchez, nothing grand, but it did the trick of overwriting Anselmo's illegitimacy, on paper at least, and in the public eye. Only the family knew, only they remembered, and it was in their own best interest to keep the secret.

Didn't that act of selflessness give The Doctor the right to discipline the child, and punish her, as he saw fit? The child *was* unruly and rebellious; he had a penchant for arson, and for tormenting the smaller children around him (though not animals, ever; he seemed to have an uncanny knack for communicating with dogs and cats and even the chickens in the coop). Maybe this was her fault, maybe she had spoiled him. As for her, well, she *was* guilty as charged (whatever the charge was). She couldn't forget the German boy, saw him in Anselmo's blue eyes every day, and reveled in the glory and the sin of her love. Through the eyes of her child her lost lover kept his hold on her heart. Her husband knew it, and vilified her—and the boy—for it.

Her father, appalled at the bruises on her face one morning he arrived unannounced, suggested she move back to the family house.

I can't, Papa.

He insisted. Her brothers would speak to The Doctor. She would never see him again.

But... what about the children?

The children—yes, *his* children, too—were to come as well. Her brothers would make sure The Doctor didn't make trouble.

That wasn't what she meant.

The Doctor's children (to Maura, although she denied it to her dying day, they were always separate from Anselmo, the fruit of her love, and of her sin) were three girls and a boy, and The Doctor was a good father to them. Never laid a hand on them. The girls, Josefina, Verónica, and Inés, he treated like porcelain dolls. Toño, the boy, was the apple of his eye. His pride and joy. She couldn't deny them their father. Family was sacred; it would be the ultimate sin to sacrifice their stability, their well-being, to her own. Even for Anselmo: having a father, no matter if only by law and not by biology, no matter how indifferent or unfatherly or even sadistic this man might be behind closed doors, guaranteed her oldest (the apple of *her* eye) a future without the stigma of bastardy. By the time Inés, the youngest, was born, Anselmo was almost a man, a strapping fifteen-year-old with the square shoulders of his (real) father. The Doctor now thought twice about raising his fists at him. If that meant Maura received double the beatings, so be it.

It was for her children. For the sanctity of Family. But I think it was more than that.

After eight years in the unwed-motherhood purgatory of shame, she understood the benefits of even a cruel husband. As The Doctor's wife she was allotted a certain standing. (The

Doctor was a respected man, not only for his ability as a physician but for his willingness to accept a sack of potatoes or two chickens when his patients were strapped for cash.) All this played a part, sure. But I think a part of her wanted the abuse.

I think she fell in love again, with her guilt this time. She welcomed the punishment, even rejoiced in it, because it made happiness impossible. She didn't deserve happiness, everyone knew it, and now God had delivered the instrument for a lifetime of penitence. As she deserved.

This was the singularity where all the reasons for leaving fell apart. What Maura lacked wasn't self-esteem but self-control. The Doctor's abuse became the punishment she deserved for the sin of having loved—the German boy, life, herself. Her guilt became an addiction, punishment the drug that satisfied it. Like some sort of twisted emotional gluttony, she couldn't get enough.

Frosting by the Forkful

Andrea Diede

The scent of cinnamon and baked bread tickles my nose. The oven door screeches open. There's a fresh batch of sticky buns. The warmth of the bakehouse melts away the crisp morning air.

I herd the children through tight aisles, navigating to our reserved table. The packed bakery rumbles, and our back corner is a refuge. The six kids squeeze around the red speckled table like any other Friday.

"Everyone has money?" I boom over the chatter. I'm as eager as they are to taste the melting sugar-frosting on each cinnamon roll. I breathe in, filling my lungs with warm air and pluck five bucks from each of their tiny hands waving the cash high above their heads. "Thank you, and you—"

They bounce up and down on the aluminum seats and chant, "CIN-NA-MON. CIN-NA-MON."

I weave back through the congestion and join the tangled line of patrons. I cross my arms over my chest and feel the bills crumple under my bicep. The line inches forward, the tip of my boot scrapes the woman's heel in front of me. She turns, glaring. I tap my foot impatiently and she turns to order at the counter.

I'm next. Thoughts of cinnamon-almond melt in my mouth.

"Yes?" the assistant scowls.

"Six cinnamon buns, extra frosting, and six milks." I shuffle through the crumpled bills warmed by the heat of my arm.

"Twenty bucks." The girl taps on the register pad, the drawer springs open.

I hand her twenty dollars and shove the rest into the pocket of my sweatpants.

"Next," she dismisses me.

I take my place in the pickup line and watch the baker plate six flaky rolls. He plunges a ladle into the tub of frosting and drenches the dough. I'm mesmerized, imagining the sugar granules dissolving on my tongue.

He shoves the tray towards me. I point to the pastry at the edge of the dish. "That cinnamon roll didn't get enough icing." The man frowns and robotically dumps frosting onto the bun.

Balancing the platter full of steaming rolls, I head back to the table. I pause and holding it up to my mouth, run my tongue along the edge of the closest sticky bun. *Mmmm.*

"Here you go."

I place the dish in the middle of the table and pass out the miniature cartons of milk.

"There's your milk, and I'll cut up your cinnamon rolls, so they'll cool faster so we—" I catch myself, "*you* can eat."

I scrape off a forkful of frosting and cram it into my mouth, then begin cutting the buns into bite-size chunks. The children fidget in their seats. Between knife slices, I stuff sweet pieces into my mouth, packing it so full I find it hard to chew.

"Mrs. Franklyn, the counselor said we're supposed to practice using our knives by ourselves," says the little blond girl raising her hand.

"Yes, she meant next week," I spit out quickly, bits of dough flying out. I fork up more frosting and steal a few more bites of a roll before placing one in front of each of the children. "Your fork is on the right side of your plates."

Some of the children use their forks, others just their fingers. I swallow a thick chunk of bread and quietly stab my fork into another child's plate of the cinnamon roll.

"Mrs. Franklyn, can you help me open my milk?" a boy asks. I snatch the milk from his hands and tear it open, swigging some of the milk to dislodge the large hunks in my mouth.

"Here you go," I return a half-empty carton of milk and cram more sticky bun into my mouth to help the children finish.

"Alright then, it's time to go now." The children stand and push in their chairs. I hand each of the children their white walking stick and they click-clack through the crowd.

Eaten

Steven Carr

Peeking between the drapes that covered her front window, Claudine stared, terrified, at the very large dark blue creature that had just walked out of the Thompson house and was now sitting on the curb of the cul de sac. It had its long legs stretched out and was tapping its large wart-covered feet together as it licked its claw-like hands with its bright red tongue. The surface of its huge belly pulsated, undulated and rippled as if whatever was inside was slowly being digested. It belched so loudly, Claudine's window shook.

When the timer on the oven chimed, she made certain the drapes were tightly closed, and then turned and ran into the kitchen. On the top of the stove four pots of different sizes sitting on the four burners, boiled, sent the aromas of vegetables, a cheese sauce, dumplings and pasta into the air. She quickly turned the burners down and as the pots simmered she opened the oven door and jabbed the twenty-pound turkey with a long two-pronged fork and licked her lips as the juices flowed from the punctures. She closed the oven door, and then rushed back into the living room.

With the volume turned down, she stood close to the television and watched the news anchor sitting behind the desk look straight into the camera and say, "That's right folks, aliens have landed and they're eating people. Nothing seems to stop them. Guns, flamethrowers, hand grenades and bazookas are useless against them. Ladies and gentlemen, we may be witnessing the beginning of the end of the human race as we are devoured by these ravenous monsters, one by one."

With the cameras still rolling, one of the creatures burst onto the news set, grabbed the news anchor and began stuffing her into its cavernous mouth as she punched, kicked and screamed. With its mouth and throat bulging from the anchor inside, it gulped, swallowing her whole. Then a test pattern flickered on. Claudine wet herself.

She ran to the window and peeked out between the drapes. The creature was gone. Just as she let out a sigh of relief, there was a loud banging on the front door.

She grabbed a porcelain vase from the stand by the window, held it above her head, and cautiously approached the door.

"Who is it?" she stammered.

"It. Is. Me. Bob," the deep voice on the other side said, enunciating each word very distinctly and in a monotone.

"I don't know anyone named Bob," she said. "What do you want?"

"I. Am. Very. Hungry," Bob said. "Do. You. Have. Any. Food?"

"No, I don't. Now go away," she said.

There was silence for a moment, and then the door splintered and the creature smashed through it.

Knocked backwards, Claudine dropped the vase and landed on the floor on her butt. "Please don't eat me!" she screamed.

The creature hovered menacingly over her for a moment, and then looked toward the kitchen. "What. Are. Those. Smells?" it said.

"I was cooking my dinner," she said, voice trembling.

"Bob. Wants. Some," it said.

"Certainly," Claudine said. "Let me serve it to you, Earth style."

As she stood up and then directed it to the dining room table, she said, "Is your name really Bob?"

"On. My. Planet. We. Are. All. Called. Bob."

* * *

The table was covered with bowls and platters heaped with food. The turkey was placed in the middle next to a gravy boat almost overflowing with thick turkey gravy.

"You don't eat until I say so," Claudine said as she sat down at one end of the table.

"Why. Not?" Bob said.

"I know you eat people like you're a glutton, but food served on a table has to be done with manners," she said.

"What. Are. Manners?"

"It's resisting your natural urges," she said.

She piled Bob's plate with food, except for turkey, and then handed it to him and then put large portions of food on her plate.

"You can eat now," she said.

As she put her fork into a dumpling, it raised its plate and slurped the food into its mouth and swallowed and then slammed the plate on the table, breaking it.

"Not. Satisfying," Bob said.

She pushed the turkey and gravy toward it. "Eat that. Maybe it will be more to your liking."

It grabbed the turkey, shoved it into its mouth and gulped it down, and then drank the gravy and tossed the gravy boat across the room, smashing it.

"That. Better," it said and then leaned back and patted its rotund stomach. "You. Big. Earth. Person. You. Eat. This. Way. All. The. Time?"

She shoveled a large forkful of spaghetti into her mouth. "Whenever I can," she said.

It belched, causing the pictures on the walls to shake, and then yawned. "I. Need. To. Sleep. Now." It yawned again. "I. Will. Eat. You. Later."

Bob got out of the chair and lay down on the floor and fell sound asleep.

Smiling, Claudine said aloud, "Nothing like turkey and gravy to knock anyone out."

She rose from her chair, and then grabbed it by its feet and dragged it into the kitchen.

* * *

When the timer went off she opened the oven door and poked the crisp outer skin of the creature with the two-pronged fork and smiled as boiled juices flowed out. She then used a small shovel and the broom handle to dig the creature's crammed body out of the oven, and laid it on a large sheet of aluminum foil spread out on the kitchen floor.

She sat on the floor next to it with a fork and knife in her hand and a napkin tied around her neck.

She then devoured him. Ravenously.

The Return of Red Ledbetter
Episode 2: The Fat Man

JP Lundstrom

"Ledbetter, wait!"

Detective Red Ledbetter waited for his partner. "What is it, Wilson?"

He watched a woman brush past, an air of exotic flowers following her.

"We're shorthanded, Slim. You interview the residents. I'll finish the two crime scenes." Wilson turned back, muttering, "Some Christmas Eve! One stiff in the alley, and another in 810."

The woman disappeared when the elevator descended.

Movement caught Ledbetter's eye. Someone behind door 809 watched and listened. The door closed without a sound.

Ledbetter rapped, and the door opened a crack, secured by a chain. A pale gray eye stared at him. "Who's there?"

"Good evening, Mrs.—"

"*Miss* Sanfte Kätzchen. You may call me Miss Kitty. And you are…?"

"Detective Ledbetter, ma'am."

"What's this about?"

"There's been an incident." He took out a small notebook. "Have you seen anything this evening?"

Her spine straightened. "I'm on the Neighborhood Watch. I see everything."

"Noticed anything unusual?"

She unhooked the chain. "Come in, Detective."

Ledbetter entered, noting the curtain pulled away from the window. Flashing lights illuminated the murder scene below.

"Do you know Mr. Peter Dick?"

"Who? You came from 810. Nobody there except Luz Apagada." She tightened the belt of her housecoat. "And the brother."

Ledbetter wrote: *brother*.

"Men coming and going at all hours. Scandalous!"

"What did you see tonight?"

She leaned closer. "You mean who!"

"Who?"

"I only caught a glimpse, but he was about five ten and a half, weight 240." She took a breath and continued. "Black hair, brown eyes, a star-shaped scar on his left eyebrow, tattoos on both arms. He was wearing a green shirt, black pants, and black shoes, size twelve."

Ledbetter wrote everything down.

"One more thing."

"What's that?"

"His shirt had a golden dragon on the back, and the words 'Chinese Food' in Mandarin. Sorry—that's all I remember."

"Thanks, ma'am."

He put his notebook away, returning to the dead woman's apartment. "Let's go, Wilson."

"You got something?"

Red relayed Miss Kitty's story.

"The Golden Dragon—I know that place. It's in Chinatown."

"Better button up—we're going out in the snow."

Wilson shivered. "Why don't you go? I'll finish the interviews."

The Golden Dragon was a classy establishment. Chinese opera music filled the air. Hammered copper topped the tables. Deferential waiters hovered.

A tall Asian woman stopped him. She wore her midnight black hair in a severe updo. The slit in her red *cheongsam* accentuated long, shapely legs.

"Good evening, sir." Blood-red lips forced a smile. Her fingernail color matched her lips. "Table for one?"

"No, thanks." Ledbetter identified himself. "I'm here to speak to your delivery man."

"I'm afraid he's out."

"When will he be back?"

She sighed impatiently. "It's hard to say."

"Try."

She watched two couples who entered. "I can't talk now, but you can speak to the owner."

She led him to a private dining room. An enormously obese man lolled before an elegantly-appointed table. "Mr. Matabang Lalaki, Detective Ledbetter wishes to speak with you."

"Thank you, Chichu." Matabang Lalaki waved an indolent hand. "Welcome, Detective."

"I'd like to ask you a few questions," Ledbetter began.

"Not right now. I'm about to enjoy Christmas Eve supper."

He gazed eagerly at the heavily-laden platters set before him.

"Ah—the appetizer course." Chopsticks in hand, he pounced, smacking his lips. "Roast suckling pig. Skin so crunchy, so tasty!"

Enraptured, he shoveled in boiled chicken livers and gizzards, joking, "A banquet without chicken is just dinner."

"Shrimp salad!" Ignoring the pop-eyed whole prawn perched on top, he dug into the white mound, grabbing first a shrimp, then a bit of lychee. He licked a glob of mayonnaise from the corner of his mouth.

"Drunken chicken?" He tasted. "No—duck, steamed in *shao xing* wine."

"Jellyfish salad." The fat man sprinkled chili sauce, then dipped into yet another platter, seizing translucent tentacles. He sighed. The sauce and a few sesame seeds clung to his lips.

"I saved this for last." His chopsticks probed a pile of jewel-like ovals the color of Coca-Cola, then popped one into his smiling mouth. "Century eggs!"

Ledbetter sprang into action. "I take it you're finished and ready to answer my questions?"

Matabang Lalaki chortled behind his napkin. "Oh, my goodness, no! That was just the end of the first course!"

"How many courses will there be?"

"Fifteen."

Ledbetter resigned himself to a long wait.

A waitress poured a cup of steaming tea. Pinkie finger raised, Lalaki sipped. "It cleanses the palate between courses."

The vegetable course contained sweet and sour squid, garlic fungus and cucumbers. Jilin Province inspired the soup, chicken with ginseng.

"Ginseng is one of the three treasures of Northeast China," Lalaki pointed out. "Very important for virility."

Indeed, he acted as professor of Chinese cuisine—his lecture accompanied every aspect of the feast. Between courses, the fat man slurped his cleansing tea.

By the time the Dimsum arrived, Ledbetter felt hungry too, but Lalaki never invited the detective to join him. One by one, the beautifully prepared dumplings disappeared between the fat man's greasy lips—*ha gau, shaomai,* and vegetable.

Alongside the Dimsum, four iconic main dishes were presented—Taiwanese beef with *sha cha,* Xinyang spicy chicken, steamed grouper with spring onions, and a seafood stir-fry, Dalian-style.

At this point, Lalaki rested, reclining on his chaise. His napkin delivered dainty pats to his lips, then his sweaty forehead. He breathed heavily, gasping for air with every word, yet he persevered.

With the rice and noodle dishes, he slowed to a more leisurely pace, capturing an errant noodle with good humor.

The thirteenth, fourteenth and fifteenth courses were brought together—dessert. The fat man's lips closed around the delicate pastry of the *tikoy,* which he pronounced without equal. Around a mouthful of *tang yuan,* he raved about having tasted Paradise. He almost got there, after choking on a bit of *baozi,* but for a quick-thinking waiter who pounded his back.

Finished at last, the gluttonous Matabang Lalaki folded his hands over his paunch.

"Now, Detective. What can I do for you?"

Cashew Nuts

Nod Ghosh

Maybe it was her dissatisfaction with her career that led my wife to overeat. Maybe it was something else. I don't know. She'd buy biscuits because I liked them. But whenever I opened the canister, there'd only be one or two left.

She devoured biscuits and cashew nuts. The house was full of cashew nuts. She was like an alcoholic, but with nuts. I'd find stashes in the bedroom, in the garage, garden shed, everywhere.

My wife had trouble bonding with our son. Perhaps she couldn't accept it wasn't him who'd made her fat. I don't know. We never talked about it. We never talked about anything really.

We'd tried for another child, but nothing happened. Maybe I only got one shot at being a father, and I got two for the price of one. My son, and the girl I had with you.

* * *

When you called me at home that evening, I kept looking over my shoulder.

"Why are you calling me here?"

The kid was running in and out of the room.

You knew I preferred to ring from work so I could talk openly, but the time difference made it hard, especially in winter when we were only eleven hours ahead. I had to go into work extra early to call you, or our girl would be in bed.

Guess it must have been a week since I last called.

"I've done it." You sounded defiant.

"What?" I was curt. *She* was in the next room.

"I've left him."

"Oh." Something leapt in my chest.

"How's the girl taking it?" I couldn't say her name out loud. *She* might hear.

"I'm seeing her every weekend."

"*Every weekend?* Where is she?"

"With him. We're trying to stay civil for her sake."

"So he stayed in the house with her?"

"Yes. I'm having another shot at my music career. I have to tour."

"But – "

"She was always closer to him."

Poor kid. Abandoned by both of us.

"What about my *access?*" I whispered the last word.

"We've talked about it."

"And?"

My son barged in again and demanded I play with him on PlayStation.

"Later mate," I said. "I'm on the phone."

"What's that?" you asked.

"Sorry *Raymond*. My son. That's all. So, what's going to happen about – *about my access to the site?*"

My wife had come into the room. She wouldn't pay attention if I were talking about work with *Raymond*.

"You can visit her there. He won't stop you. You partly own the house anyway."

Yes. And my money was tied up in a place where you no longer lived.

158

"Look I'll call you later," I said. "I have to go."

* * *

When I visited you in the spring, we were free. No more sneaky kisses, or stolen romps in rent-by-the-hour hotels. No more husband. You openly paraded me as your partner. You just didn't tell your friends I had a wife and son back home.

I visited you more frequently. I saw our girl. You wanted to take things further.

"We've found each other again," your voice was soft, but firm. "Let's make a proper go of it. Come back and live here."

I was aware that your music wasn't going to make it in the late nineties techno-dominated scene. But you couldn't see it. So you chipped away with your folksy singer-songwriter genre, touring, supporting aging rockers. You weren't prepared to give up.

"I have a good life. I'd never find another job that paid as much." I said. "You should join me."

"Not until you leave that cunt of a wife of yours," you snarled.

"I have to wait for the right time. Joe's still young."

"Then what, you want me to come and be your part time whore?"

"I never said that."

"*Our daughter's* still young," you said. "*I* can't leave her. And I'm not coming unless you leave that bitch."

I understood the animosity between you and my wife. After all, you'd both wanted me once, several years ago. And I'd wanted you both, but that would have been impossible. Impossible and greedy. She'd been beautiful when she came away with me. The obvious choice. And I'd had to create the illusion I'd chosen just one of you.

"I'm not leaving Joe."

I couldn't leave my boy. He was a troubled child. So I carried on with my sham of a marriage.

* * *

My wife has changed. Her obesity is a real turn-off. I find her repulsive. Joe is increasingly surly and disrespectful towards her. I admit I'm not supportive. I indulge him, and take his side in arguments. The boy and I go on our male-bonding camping trips, do our thing. She stays at home.

She's started mixing with some strange people. She stays out late, meets a load of wackos. People with names like Aruna, Surya and Krystal.

It suits me. Gives me the opportunity to phone you and speak freely.

* * *

My wife recently got herself a tattoo. I came back from that 'conference', and there it was, an eyeball thing on her arm.

"What's that?" I asked.

"What does it look like?"

I wondered how much it had cost. "A tattoo, but I can't make out what it is." If she had to have a tattoo, why not a rose or anchor or something? Not this thing that looked like an incomplete eyeball.

"It's therapeutic," she said. "It's to help me grow as a person."

Shit. She didn't need to grow any bigger.

"You know we can't waste money," I said. I needed to get another grand to you by Wednesday.

"You have no idea," my wife said. "Really. You have no idea at all."

She sank her hand into the bowl on the coffee table, and crammed her mouth full of cashew nuts.

The tattoo wobbled, red and raised on the loose flesh of her arm, and I thought again of how I'd rather be with you.

Another Kind of Surprise Party

Paul Beckman

This year the party's at Eddie's and he promised to give us a theme soon after we arrive. I was pouring a Jameson's neat for myself and a Pinot Noir for Elaine when Eddie slow-walked up and handed me a small brown envelope with my name written by a calligrapher on it—just my name and not Elaine's. In return I handed him an envelope with ten $100 bills which was the entry fee for this year's party.

Open it. Elaine pushed. Hurry and open it, I can't wait to see what this party's all about.

I opened. Slid out a card beautifully written by the same calligrapher and showed it to Elaine.

> Welcome to our party. This year's theme is the Seven Deadly Sins. Mirsky—yours is gluttony and starts at this party and goes for two weeks to our vacation planning dinner party. Remember, this is not to be shared with anyone until the dinner party a fortnight from now.
>
> Your host,
> Eddie

Elaine looked at Mirsky, closed her eyes and shook her head as he grabbed the bottle of Jameson's and filled his glass. Then he reached into a container of martini olives—grabbed a handful and began popping them into his mouth like he would peanuts, after first shaking them in his hand. Next he started in on the maraschino cherries and left a small pile of stems and walked into the living room where the other members of his club were mingling.

Mirsky was filling his pocket with nonpareils when he noticed Fred walk up behind Elaine, kiss her on the neck and grab a handful of ass. Elaine turned around, put her arms around Fred's neck but dashed his hopes by pouring her remaining Pinot on his head.

Someone brought Fred a towel and he walked into the bathroom after glaring at Mirsky and made himself as presentable as possible.

Elaine looked around for Mirsky and found him in the kitchen raiding the refrigerator. She took the turkey drumstick from his hand and pulled it out of his mouth and returned it to the refrigerator.

Mirsky liked his license to be a glutton and Elaine hated it. She had convinced him two years ago to eat healthy and he'd be healthy. Now it's all gone to hell.

At dinnertime Elaine was seated between Fred and Eddie and Mirsky between Babs (Eddie's wife) and Rona, Fred's wife.

"Say, Rona, are you going to eat your Brussels sprouts?"

"Help yourself," Rona said and as Mirsky was helping himself so was Rona. She deftly unzipped Mirsky's pants and slipped her hand in and was holding his balls. "Good tradeoff, don't you think?" Rona asked as Mirsky popped the last four Brussels sprouts in his mouth and reached down and removed her hand and zipped back up. She was obviously in on Fred's Lust selection.

For dessert Eddie and Babs put out miniature Italian pastries and a few kinds of gelato. Mirsky bypassed the dessert plates and left for the kitchen coming back with a clean dinner plate which he piled high with cannolis, Napoleons, pasticiotti, sfogliatelle, and biscotti. He also filled his breast pocket with biscotti while he was on his third cup of espresso.

Mirsky belched and farted all the way to his car while Elaine led the way staying upwind. She got on his case saying, "There's gluttony and there's gluttony and you brought gluttony to a whole new level."

For the next two weeks Mirsky ate grinders or pizza for lunch, pasta dishes for dinner, and always had at least one dessert. His weight ballooned and he couldn't button his pants or his shirt collar. He brought himself some new clothes, a couple of watches and a case of Jameson's for the house. He drank a bottle of wine with his dinner and then retired to his recliner with the Jameson's bottle and a tin of Danish Butter Cookies.

After two weeks passed the group got together at Eddie's house again. There were stacks of $100 bills on the bar. He started with Gluttony. Eddie brought out his bathroom scale and five men lined up to weigh in.

Mirsky got on the scale first and in two weeks he'd gained 38 1/2 pounds. He turned to the others, patted his gut, and proudly wished them luck. The other men bowed down to Mirsky and congratulated him on being the biggest glutton in the room—especially since the others weren't trying to gain but went on the South Beach Diet. Once again Mirsky was their foil and once again he heard about it from Elaine on the way home.

The Full Platter

Abha Iyengar

Leo's stomach needed lipo-sucking again. He would emerge from this and restrict his diet for a few months, and then he would begin sliding again. He enjoyed cooking and hosting parties where people ate the food, smacked their mouths in delighted appreciation and licked their fingers and plates clean. He also enjoyed eating the meals he cooked. So when he had to just eat a couple of spoons of the meals he served, while his friends ate by the mouthful, his heart died and his stomach roiled with unsatisfied gastric juices. Eventually he had to succumb. And when he did, he went the whole hog, piling up plate after plate with fish and meat and butter and eggs and mayonnaise-drenched salads, everything that was a no for him if he had to maintain his slimmer stomach profile. And then when he sagged once more over his belt, he returned for the next lipo-suction. This was the fourth one. The doctor had advised him not to have any more surgeries done after this one, as scar tissue had built up to a great extent. It was safer to just eat less, to be more in control.

Leo had looked at the doctor with his brown puppy-dog eyes (people said that was his best feature), and asked, "Doctor, what else is there to live for, if not food?"

The doctor had no answer. He was a wise man and knew that each one had his way of keeping sane and happy, and for Leo it translated into food; lots of food that filled not only the vacuum in his stomach but other hungers too, but the doctor did not want to go there. He had enough on his platter, dealing every day with cases like Leo. Though Leo's eyes were young, his body was hurtling downhill, and he could only help in applying the brakes. Beyond that, he could do nothing.

He patted Leo's shoulder and said, "Take it easy, son, just take it easy. Use food as fuel, nothing more." But he knew his words would fall on deaf ears; the only voice that made sense to Leo was his stomach's hungry rumble.

Gluttony

Michael Webb

I see an area of my right big toenail where the polish has chipped. The chipped area forms a shape that looks like a heart. Behind my feet, the television is on. A brown-skinned woman is serving something hot into a paper cup, and a bald, heavy-set man takes the cup and samples from it with a white plastic spoon. The volume is low, but I can tell from his expression that he is telling the woman that it is delicious. The bald man is heavy-set, as you might expect someone on a food show to be. I wonder if the steaming broth he is making a show of loving really satisfies him. I don't know why I watch food shows, when they only make me hungry, but I do.

I am not sleeping. This happens to me when he is on duty overnight. I know harm can come to him any time, but the night is more terrifying and mysterious. I've never slept well, but when I know he is working, it is especially hard to rest. I also know work shifts are sometimes a moment when he can come to me, his slim face dark with shadows of stubble and need, and I can satisfy him, moving quickly to sate him, top him off, allow him a moment of release amid all the agony and selfishness and human wreckage he deals with.

I know he's married. I don't hate her, which is something that surprised me when I realized it. I see her sometimes, at Target or walking their five-year old across the street from the bus stop, and I feel a sort of distant pity for her, the belly that was probably once baby weight and is now just there, hanging above her too tight jeans. I have always hated women who do what I do, women who cheat, who take what belongs to another female and use their hips and legs and breasts and lips to seduce the men who are too dumb to say no. It is insulting to men to feel that way, to see them as beasts who can't help themselves, but I did, until I became one of those people I had always despised.

    I try not to think about the rest of him, the father and husband, the respected, polite officer of the law. It is simpler for me to see him as body, as desire, as abs and thighs and strong back and bobbing erect cock, as force, as grunting, sweaty, groaning flesh, on top of me or in my hungry mouth. He mentions her sometimes, and I always steer the conversation, when there is any, in another direction, anywhere that won't remind me of the fact that, while he may be breathing beside me in the darkness, his fluids drying on my skin, he will eventually go home to someone else.

    I know that, if I were to see his polished face on the news, followed by one of those sad pictures with the tiny yellow tags marking where the bullet shells were found, and then the next week seeing the marching wave of blue suits, row after awful row, with the keening wail of a bagpipe, that no one would weep for me. It would be her, unsteady in a black dress, supported by a brother or an uncle, on the screen, the whole region seeing her pain, imagining her loss, crying for her emptiness, while I sob alone.

    I understand I'm being selfish. There are lots of men, tall ones and short ones, thin ones and fat ones, handsome ones and homely ones, and surely the world contains one, probably more than one, who would give me what I want, the wordless, stringless, no commitment physical release, the coming, and then the leaving. The world is full of danger, an uncertain place. An end could come at any time, for me, for him, for the bald man on the TV. I want what I want, staring past my imperfect toes, waiting for him, my own need like a meal I can never finish eating.

You Gonna Eat That?

Wayne Scheer

Larry Turner loved to eat. He'd dive into a bowl of pasta like a ten-year old kid in a swimming pool. Slurping and splashing, he'd come up for air, occasionally let out an "ahhh," and jump back in.

As a child, he'd visit his grandmother and entertain the family by devouring huge piles of corn beef and cabbage while always saving room for dessert. As a teenager, Larry's food consumption approached myth. He even won a fried chicken-eating contest his freshman year in college.

But now, as he neared forty, his eating antics had become a source of embarrassment for his wife and children. Kathy, his nine-year old, would say, "Daddy, stop making those noises when you eat," and David, at seven, looked at his father with a combination of awe and shame, realizing that he could never fill his father's seat at the dining table.

"You gonna eat that?" Larry would ask no one in particular as he pointed to most anything not actually in someone's mouth.

But the fates played him a cruel trick. During a routine physical exam, Larry heard the words every middle-aged man dreads. "Mr. Turner," the doctor said. "You are a heart attack waiting to happen. You must lose weight and lower your cholesterol."

Larry imagined sharing a salad with his family instead of a large double cheese pizza with pepperoni and sausage; he thought of what it would be like eating desserts of fresh fruit instead of fruit pies.

Larry's wife, Lois, tried hard not to show her exhilaration when he tearfully declared he was going to have to diet. She prepared dinners of stir-fried vegetables over rice, but the rice was brown and she limited him to one portion. He found grilled salmon with steamed vegetables delicious, but the French bread and butter he usually devoured was nowhere to be found.

And desserts really did consist of fresh fruit.

Larry no longer looked forward to meals with the enthusiasm of the family schnauzer, but he told himself his health and his family's welfare meant more to him than ribs smothered in sauce with piles of fries, hush puppies and coleslaw.

Reluctantly, he kept to his diet and lost twenty pounds. Six months later, his doctor declared his cholesterol count had decreased significantly. "Keep doing what you're doing," the doctor said.

But Larry's first thought was to celebrate with a good meal.

"Lois, I've worked hard. We have to go out for a steak dinner."

Lois agreed, until he added, "And not to a good steakhouse with tiny portions of aged beef and vegetables with French names. I want to go to *Here's the Beef*."

She cringed. Thinking it best not to expose the children to the spectacle of Daddy falling off the (chuck) wagon, she decided to leave the children home.

Upon entering the restaurant, they were assaulted by the odor of burning flesh. Larry inhaled like a madman. The sight of people eating huge piles of meat and baked potatoes piled high with sour cream made him salivate more than Pavlov's dog.

He ordered the Dead Man Walking porterhouse. "Just pass it over the grill. I want to hear it moo when I bite into it. And give me a double order of fries with that. And onion rings."

Lois, glaring at her husband, ordered the grilled snapper, steamed vegetables and rice.

They sat at a wooden table in the middle of a steakhouse filled with gluttonous carnivores. Six varieties of steak sauce served as a centerpiece. Soon he was served a slab of beef the size of a deflated basketball. Fries were piled so high he could barely see his wife who sat across from him.

Larry's eyes bulged and his heart pounded. Hands trembling, he picked up his knife with Jack-the-Ripper enthusiasm, and cut into the thick, red beef. Blood spurted and dripped as he shoveled the meat into his open mouth.

"Ummm," he said. "Ahhh."

Lois, determined to let Larry experience his gastric orgy without comment, watched as Larry devoured his food like a starving animal. She loved her husband and wanted him happy, so she forced herself to smile. Despite her discomfort, she ate her snapper and made polite conversation as he continued to wolf down his supper.

But when he reached across to her, pointed to her roll and asked, "You gonna eat that?" she could hold back her emotion no longer. Her face flushed and her hands trembled as she stabbed the back of his hand with her fork.

Also from Pure Slush Books

https://pureslush.com/store/

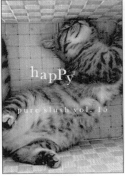

- Lust 7 Deadly Sins Vol. 1
  ISBN: 978-1-925536-47-8 (paperback) / 978-1-925536-48-5 (eBook)
- Happy² Pure Slush Vol. 15
  ISBN: 978-1-925536-39-3 (paperback) / 978-1-925536-40-9 (eBook)
- Inane Pure Slush Vol. 14
  ISBN: 978-1-925536-17-1 (paperback) / 978-1-925536-18-8 (eBook)
- Freak Pure Slush Vol. 13
  ISBN: 978-1-925536-15-7 (paperback) / 978-1-925536-16-4 (eBook)
- Summer Pure Slush Vol. 12
  ISBN: 978-1-925536-13-3 (paperback) / 978-1-925536-14-0 (eBook)
- tall…ish Pure Slush Vol. 11
  ISBN: 978-1-925101-80-5 (paperback) / 978-1-925101-98-0 (eBook)